"I have no idea why we care so much, but we do. My parents love you. I love you. And——"

Clemmie broke off her spiel when she realized what she'd just admitted. Her mouth dropped open at her slip, her face flaming with humiliation. She whirled around and fled out the door.

In shock, she heard his steps pound behind her, closing in on her, right before he grabbed her waist. His other hand then found her arm, and he spun her around to face him. "Oh no, Clemmie. You're not getting away that easy." He grabbed both her arms, and she thought he might shake her. "I want some answers. And I won't take 'later' or 'soon' this time!"

D1111610

PAMELA GRIFFIN lives in Texas and divides her time among family, church activities, and writing. She fully gave her life to the Lord in 1988 after a rebellious young adulthood and owes the fact that she's still alive today to an all-loving, forgiving God and a mother who prayed that her wayward daughter would come "home." Pamela's main goal in writing Christian romance is to encourage others through entertaining stories that also heal the wounded spirit. Please visit Pamela at: www.Pamela-Griffin.com.

Books by Pamela Griffin

HEARTSONG PRESENTS

Don't miss out on any of our super romances. Write to us at the following address for information on our newest releases and club information.

Heartsong Presents Readers' Service
PO Box 721
Uhrichsville, OH 44683

Or visit www.heartsongpresents.com

In Search of a Dream

Pamela Griffin

Heartsong Presents

A huge thank-you to my critique partners, Theo and Mom. And to my Lord, who removed the scales from my eyes so that I could see truth, I owe everything.

A note from the Author:
I love to hear from my readers! You may correspond with me by writing:

Pamela Griffin
Author Relations
PO Box 721
Uhrichsville, OH 44683

ISBN 978-1-60260-881-8

IN SEARCH OF A DREAM

Copyright © 2010 by Pamela Griffin. All rights reserved. Except for use in any review, the reproduction or utilization of this work in whole or in part in any form by any electronic, mechanical, or other means, now known or hereafter invented, is forbidden without the permission of Heartsong Presents, an imprint of Barbour Publishing, Inc., PO Box 721, Uhrichsville, Ohio 44683.

All of the characters and events in this book are fictitious. Any resemblance to actual persons, living or dead, or to actual events is purely coincidental.

Our mission is to publish and distribute inspirational products offering exceptional value and biblical encouragement to the masses.

PRINTED IN THE U.S.A.

prologue

Lyons' Refuge, 1937

Clemmie Lyons toiled over her letter, her mind elsewhere, her heart playing betrayer with thoughts of. . .

Him. . .

Her dream. . .

A dream no longer. . .

"Stop it," she chastised herself. "It's been more than three years. He has his own life, a different life."

He had a life all right; one that evidently didn't include acknowledgment of her or her parents, who had practically raised him on their farm. They'd received not one call, not one letter or lousy word that he was still living and breathing. She knew he must be; they would have heard otherwise, since the navy informed next of kin. His mother died giving him life; his father died in jail. He had no living relatives. Was he even still in the armed forces? It had been more than seven years since he entered them.

Clemmie blew out a frustrated breath and put pen to paper:

> *Really, Hannah, your offer for me to come visit couldn't have come at a better time.*

At least with such a diversion, Clemmie would be away from Lyons' Refuge and all the persistent memories that nagged at her. She shook her head and went back to writing her letter:

> *Things aren't hopeless here, despite the depression, since Grandfather didn't invest in stocks, but I look forward to a change of scenery, regardless. It's very gracious of your*

*great-uncle to allow me to visit his estate for the rest of
the summer. How fortunate that he also protected his
investments and didn't lose everything on that horrible
Black Friday.*

And maybe, if she did go to Connecticut, *his* face wouldn't
haunt her from every corner of the house!

*Did I tell you we received a letter from Angel? She and
her husband are well, as is little Everett. I remember when
I learned that Roland was Vittorio Piccoli's grandson I
questioned Angel's logic and sanity! But after visiting with
them last summer, I can see why Angel is infatuated. He's
very nice. I'm sure I don't need to tell you what a monster his
grandfather is, since he was the mastermind in the tragedy
that befell your parents, with the loss of their first child and
almost killing your mother! How terrible those days must
have been for them!*

*But I digress; Tommy went to live at their farm two
years ago, to help out—I think I told you? However, that's
not all—he's fallen in love! Can you believe it? Our little
Tommy? Strangely enough, it's with Angel's cousin, Faye,
who's been a frequent visitor to the farm. They were married
last month. We only learned news of it when Angel thought to
write us. I'm so thankful she did! Tommy was always such a
horrible letter writer, much like Father.*

And very much like Joel Litton.

Clemmie curbed the desire to throw her fountain pen
across the room. Her behavior really was absurd. She'd barely
thought of him these past years—well, not as often as in her
childhood anyway. She'd been all of ten when he entered the
navy. And on his last visit home, near her fifteenth birthday,
he'd had a girl hanging on his arm. Clemmie scrunched up
her nose in distaste at the memory, but a faint smile soon
tilted her lips.

Despite his being twelve years older and quite obviously the man about town—a true heartbreaker, from all the unattached young women she'd seen panting after him—Joel always had made time for Clemmie. He treated her as a kid sister, and his annoying habit of calling her "Carrottop" rankled, the older she grew. But even if he did tease, she tolerated such behavior to be near him. All the boys had teased her, but Joel had also shown kindness. He'd acted as if he enjoyed her sole company, what little of it she scrounged from his clinging female companions, and had treated her as if she mattered. Was it any wonder that she had developed a hopeless fascination for him as a child?

He'd been a true scoundrel and the original ringmaster of troublemakers at Lyons' Refuge when her father first started the reform school. Joel had been a trial and a terror, in direct opposition to his angelic looks. Perhaps, in part, it was his wildness and devil-may-care attitude that had been the attraction for her then. Added to that, his princely features and heavenly blue eyes. . .

"Stop it, Clemmie! This is getting you nowhere fast!"

She threw the closed pen on the coverlet, congratulating herself that she didn't send it smacking into the wall. Such half-buried memories wouldn't be torturing her if she hadn't run across a box of Joel's things while looking through her trunk for items to pack. He'd entrusted her with his box of boyhood trinkets before he went into the service, in an effort to stem her tears at his departure.

"There, there, Clemmie," he'd soothed, his hand going under her chin, his other wiping her eyes with his handkerchief. "It's not like I'll be gone forever, sweetheart. I'll be back soon enough."

But not to stay.

And obviously those few paltry furloughs home were to be the sum total of his appearances, thus ending his life and time at the refuge.

Yes, a summer in Connecticut was looking better and better.

"You look rather like a dog in the manger."

Clemmie started at the teasing voice that also held a note of concern. She realized she'd left her door ajar and turned to look at the dear woman who cooked for everyone at Lyons' Refuge. She wasn't her aunt by relation, but Clemmie regarded the sprightly woman as close to being one and addressed her as such.

"Aunt Darcy." Clemmie wondered what she'd heard of her little outburst and how long she'd been standing there. "I didn't hear you come up."

Darcy moved into the room, worry lines marking her usually smooth brow. Youth could no longer claim her, but the only evidence of age were the silvering hairs among the dark ones crowning her temple. "What's got you so upset, luv?"

She sat next to Clemmie, her gaze taking in the unfinished letter then straying to the cigar box Clemmie had beside her. No one at the refuge smoked; it wasn't allowed, and Clemmie wondered where Joel had found the box. Probably from her grandfather who did smoke, to Mama's consternation. Clemmie prevented her hand from straying to the box, hoping Darcy wouldn't realize whose items it contained.

"I'm just in a melancholy mood. Late spring fever in the early summer, perhaps." She tried for an offhand smile.

Darcy cocked her brow. "It wouldn't have anything to do with you leaving, would it? You don't have to go. Things aren't so bad we can't manage. With your grandfather's aid and other supporters, we do quite well, I daresay." Her smile lit the room, chasing away the clouds that had settled on Clemmie's spirit.

"I know. But I *want* to see Hannah. We were closest in age, and I miss her. It's been years. But. . .well, it's my first time to step foot away from home. Ever." Even during the outings her parents sometimes took with Darcy to New York City, the children always were left behind under the watchful eye of Brent—Darcy's husband and the schoolmaster.

"A bit nervous, luv?" Darcy put a hand to Clemmie's chin.

"You're a big girl now. Aye—more'n that. A young lady! Coo! I never thought I'd see the day. And I think it's a good thing for you to see a bit of the world."

"I feel guilty leaving when I know Mama depends on my help with the smaller children."

"You shouldn't feel the blame—none at all! You're long overdue for a treat, and there's plenty living here at the farm to help out."

"I agree with Darcy."

Clemmie turned toward the doorway and smiled at the woman whose looks she favored. She only hoped her hair darkened to the beautiful auburn of her mother's, now sprinkled with gray. Strange how while she favored her beautiful mother, Clemmie felt so plain.

"Don't feel that you should stay, dear." Her mother moved the cigar box and took the space on the other side of Clemmie. "If you don't want to go, that's one thing, and you mustn't feel obligated. But it would be a golden opportunity for you to spread your wings. I fear, with you being my firstborn, I've coddled you severely. Your father would agree."

Clemmie wrapped her arm around her mother's waist. "I don't mind, Mama."

"Would you like to go see Hannah?"

Clemmie nodded.

"Then go with my blessing."

A stampede of running footsteps clambered upstairs, making all three women face the door, where Darcy's two youngest sons came to a sudden awkward stop, bumping into one another and almost falling.

"Mama! Aunt Charleigh! Come quick," Roger blurted out. "That new boy is making trouble again. They're outside fighting!"

"He gave Adam a bloody nose," young Matthew piped up, almost gleefully.

"And Adam gave him a black eye."

"The other boys are taking bets on who'll win this time."

Her mother and Darcy exchanged long-suffering glances and quickly rose. "Go tell your father and Uncle Stewart."

"Yes, Aunt Charleigh!"

"And don't you dare be gettin' in on the gamble!"

"Yes, Mama!"

The two boys disappeared.

"He's a terror, that one," Darcy mused.

"Quentin is no worse than any other boys we've handled. Do you recall the fistfights Joel and Herbert used to get into?" At the mention of Joel, a brief, worried silence ensued as it so often did. "And then there was Clint and anyone who looked at him cross-eyed, be it boy or girl," her mother added quickly. "I still think it a wonder that he and Miranda are now married."

"Aye," Darcy said on a laugh mixed with a groan. "Those were days unforgettable. And you, Charleigh, always ready to tackle the impossible."

Her mother laughed. "You're one to talk! You were and still are the first into the fray—to jump at any unconventional new idea. Remember your initial endeavors to bring order to the refuge? The fence painting contest and the trip to the carnival?"

"I suppose I'm a bit gung ho at that. Brent tells me the same... though it didn't turn out all bad. I wound up getting him in the bargain." Darcy winked, and both women chuckled. "Time's a wastin', and I'm for certain both our men'll need help issuing order among that brood, once they take care of those two rapscallions."

"We'll talk more about your visit after dinner," her mother assured Clemmie.

Watching them go, Clemmie shook her head and smiled in wistful contemplation.

Just another crazy, mixed-up day at the refuge.

She would miss her home and family, even miss the daily chaos that went hand in hand with keeping, raising, and reforming young hoodlums, as strange as that seemed. But

Mother was right. And after hearing Joel's name mentioned, she realized that if she was ever to embark on her own life, she needed to get as far away from memories of him as possible. At least for a little while.

For Clemmie, the time had come to grow up and put childish dreams far behind her.

one

Clemmie stepped off the train, holding in a nervous breath. With wide eyes, she scanned the crowded platform of lively passengers, eager to spot a familiar face. She'd rarely left the farm in her entire life, and then no farther than a few miles' drive—to church, to her grandfather's estate, to the central hub of their small town. The hustle and bustle of passengers leaving from and coming to this strange station unsettled her, much as it had in Ithaca, only there she'd had her parents' company before her train departed.

Here, she was all alone.

She almost bit a hole through her lip before she caught sight of Hannah Thomas's shining black hair and piercing blue-gray eyes. As pretty as ever, her friend waved and ran forward to greet her. The girls met halfway in a warm hug.

"I thought your train would never get here! You know me—so impatient." Hannah laughed and hugged her again. "Oh, it's so good to see you, Clemmie! It's been ages and ages. I enjoy your letters, but togetherness is so much nicer, don't you agree? I see your hair has gotten darker—you were right. And I think your freckles faded, too. Me, I can't tolerate the sun, though Mama's half-Polynesian. But I inherited my fair skin from Papa's side of the family. Still it's nothing like Bette Davis's. I have photographs of her and other movie stars in my photo box—I'll show you when we get home. Some of them are even signed! Oh, but listen to me carrying on! How's everyone at the refuge? Are they well? I can't believe it's been *years* since I've seen most of them!"

In her excitement, Hannah bounced from one subject to another like a runaway ball, and Clemmie smiled. It was nice to see some things never changed.

"Everyone's well. They send their love. And you have the prettiest skin I've ever seen, so don't complain." And Hannah did. Flawless, without a freckle to mar it. Hannah also blushed prettily, like a pink rose, unlike Clemmie, who resembled something less attractive, like a tomato.

"You're sweet to say so." Hannah gave her a dimpled smile. "Oh look, there's Papa! I was too excited to wait and ran ahead." She grabbed Clemmie's arm, pulling her along toward Bill Thomas, Brent's brother. Clemmie marveled how the two men could be twins, though Hannah's father looked more like an outdoorsman, solid in physique with stronger, defined features.

"Wait," Clemmie said with a laugh. "My luggage!"

"Oh—sorry!" Hannah giggled. "I'm just so excited to finally have you with us."

Hannah's father met them at the baggage car with a warm welcome for Clemmie and retrieved her luggage. Trailing her father, who toted both bags, Hannah filled Clemmie in on as much as she could in the short distance they had to walk.

". . .Mama has a picnic planned after church Sunday. Everyone will be there. You might see Herbert, too. He and his wife go to our church and—"

"Wait—what?" Clemmie stopped midstep and turned to Hannah.

"Herbert Miller. From the refuge."

"Herbert and his wife live in Cedarbrook?" she asked in amazement.

"I thought you knew. When he quit working for my father and got that job at the paper, he met Thea. They had planned to move to where her family now lives—in Maine."

"That much I knew. They decided to stay?"

"Yes. Since the house is bought and paid for, it gives them a sure place to live. It's small, but they seem to like it. I think it once belonged to a member of her family. I heard the story but can't remember details." Hannah gave an unconcerned toss of her head. "They don't live far from my uncle's. Within cycling distance. You could pay her a call if you like. She must be lonely since she has only her two little girls to talk to all day while Herbert's at work."

Clemmie didn't ask why Hannah never visited Thea. Her fifteen-year-old cousin, sweet as she could be, had a touch of snobbishness, though she wasn't unkind. Her few faults aside, Hannah made a good friend, and Clemmie had her own batch of shortcomings so knew better than to judge anyone.

Once the chauffeur pulled the Rolls Royce into the winding drive of the estate, Clemmie's eyes widened theatrically. Having the chauffeur waiting at the car and opening the doors for them had been bizarre enough. She'd never had a stranger wait on her before. But this. . .she felt almost like a princess or maybe a pauper coming to abide at a fairy-tale castle.

Lyons' Refuge was big—it had to be with all the children her parents housed—but this home was majestic, a haven for the wealthy, bigger than her grandfather's manor. Round turrets flanked both ends of the pale stone dwelling, the architectural design of the house medieval. Pink roses and ivy climbed the walls. The arched window above the double front doors was composed of so many different shades of glass that in the sunlight, it glowed with iridescence.

"My great-uncle has a thing for the late Middle Ages and the Renaissance. He had the house designed. Wait till you see the inside!"

The inside of the monolith reflected its exterior grandeur. Clemmie's mouth dropped open in amazement, and Hannah giggled. "He isn't home much, what with his canned tuna business and constant business trips. He isn't home now. Just Mama and the rest of the family."

A beautiful woman with glossy black hair and exotic features glided into the foyer. Her skin was still incredibly smooth, her hair not silvered one iota. She looked like she could be Hannah's sister, though Clemmie knew this was Sarah, her mother. She wore a common, blue cotton dress, seeming out of place in so fine a home, but her manner was regal.

"Clemmie," she said, smiling and moving forward to hug her. "It's so nice to have you come stay with us."

"Thank you for inviting me, Mrs. Thomas."

She smiled. "And your family? They are well?"

"Yes, they send their love."

The remainder of the evening passed smoothly. Hannah's brothers and sisters were quiet, nowhere near as boisterous as the children at the refuge, including Clemmie's own siblings. She wondered if they were on their best behavior or if they always acted docile and well behaved. After supper she went upstairs to the room she'd been given. Her friend appeared at the door, just as Clemmie put the last of her things away.

"Oh, Clemmie." Hannah dropped to the bed in a foul temper. "I forgot I promised Mama I'd help her catalog items for the bazaar. She just reminded me. It's such a bore, and I don't want to burden you by asking you to come along on your first real day here. But I hate to leave you alone. I'll be gone at least four hours every afternoon. It's dreadfully tedious work. So many donations." She sighed. "But I promised."

Clemmie was awful at itemizing and categorizing. She feared that if she did offer her aid, she'd be more hindrance than help. "I don't mind having some time to myself." She pondered an idea. "If you give me directions to Thea's, perhaps I can visit while you're at the bazaar."

"That's a marvelous idea! Then I know you'll be entertained. It's easy to find their house. They live a few miles from here. I'll loan you my bicycle."

Clemmie thought about her uncoordinated lower limbs. "I prefer to walk."

"Walk?" Hannah regarded her as if the word were foreign to her vocabulary.

Clemmie laughed. "It's okay. On the farm I do a lot of it."

So mentally armed with directions and eager for a chat with Herbert's wife, Clemmie set out the next day for a visit. The air felt bracing though tolerable, the neighborhood opulent. The farther she walked, the more crowded and less flagrant the houses appeared, more like she felt real homes ought to look.

Coming upon a quaint house beyond a short picket fence, Clemmie reasoned this must be Herbert's residence since it was the only blue-shuttered house on the street. An abandoned pile of wooden blocks sat to one side of the porch, waiting for their small owner's return. Somewhere a dog barked, and bees hummed from nearby hydrangea bushes.

Clemmie straightened her hair, her blouse, and her skirt then rang the bell. She ought to have called first, but Hannah didn't know the number or if the Millers even owned a phone. That seemed strange to Clemmie; her father had installed a telephone at Lyons' Refuge when they first were made available to residential homes, though since they ran a children's reformatory, the expense had been not only helpful but also necessary.

The door opened. A short, pretty, brown-haired woman with a weary smile and welcoming eyes looked at her.

"Hello?"

"Hi, Thea. You might not remember me, but I was at your wedding. I'm Clemmie Lyons, Charleigh and Stewart's daughter. From the refuge."

Thea's eyes grew wide. At first Clemmie thought she saw alarm but decided it must have been from the eyes adjusting to the bright sunlight, since Thea then smiled.

"Of course I remember you. Herbert talks about his days there all the time." She hesitated. "Do come in. He's at work at the newspaper office, and it's just me and Loretta. Bethany's at school."

"Hello there." Clemmie smiled at the little girl, who peered shyly up behind her mother's skirts. "What a pretty dolly you have."

Loretta smiled bashfully. Clemmie at once felt a bond with Loretta, seeing the little girl's head of bright copper red hair.

Thea led Clemmie inside, to the back of the house and the kitchen. Their home was cheery, not neat as a pin like the mansion she'd just left, what with bits of evidence here and there that this place housed two little girls. But it was inviting and warm, like the refuge. Only Thea's manner seemed distant, as she darted an anxious glance out a window facing the backyard.

"Would you like some refreshment? I'll make coffee." Thea stopped suddenly, her hand on the scoop in the coffee grounds. "You do like coffee?"

"Coffee sounds wonderful." Clemmie felt awkward. "Did I come at a bad time? I could return later."

"What. . . ?" Thea looked at her again, distracted. "No. Now is fine. It's nearing noon, and Herbert should be home for lunch unless things at the paper are busy. But you're welcome to stay."

Her words were gracious, only her tone didn't sound welcoming. The sudden reverberations of a bell proved that Herbert did own a phone. "I'll just be a minute." Thea hurried from the sideboard and disappeared into the hall.

Loretta watched from the doorway, creeping closer to Clemmie. The girl's bashfulness dissolved into delight as she glanced at the window.

"Kitty!" she pointed, with a sunny smile at Clemmie, then darted for the door.

Clemmie had a glimpse of orange fur shooting away from the pane before Loretta flung open the door and raced outside.

Clemmie paused only a moment before going after her. The child, she knew, was only three and too young to be left outside on her own. Clemmie's lifetime of experience looking after her brothers and sisters told her that much.

"See my kitty?" Loretta asked Clemmie with delight. An orange tabby evaded Loretta's small, chubby hands as the child pounced. The kitten scampered toward a shed a short distance away, or rather what looked like a shed at first glance. Clemmie noticed a chair sitting on boards that formed a short porch under an overhang, all of it enclosed by a railing. A few abandoned toys lay near the wall. Perhaps it was the children's playhouse, though it seemed too big for that.

All interest in the whereabouts of the cat forgotten, Clemmie watched the door to the small dwelling open and a man step into the shadow of the overhang. She squinted through the glare of the sun, trying to get a good look at him as she drew close. His hair was fair, not red, so it couldn't be Herbert, and he stood tall and slender, not short like Thea's husband. He stepped out farther, crossing the line of shadow into sunlight.

Clemmie's heart seemed to stop beating. She felt dizzy, as if she might swoon, and experienced a rush of energy at the same time.

"Loretta? Is that you?" His piercing blue eyes looked in Clemmie's direction, staring at her as if reaching deep into her soul. She stood rooted to the spot, unable to move if a brush fire started beneath her feet. "Tell me that blasted cat isn't on the loose and under my feet again, ready to trip me."

Joel!

There was no mistaking his identity; his face, though slightly altered with time and bearing a scruffy mustache and beard, had been imprinted on her memory for years, aided by yearly photographs her mother had organized for those who lived at the refuge. The man from whom she had yearned even one word of communication or the barest glimpse now stood before her in the flesh, with only the length of several grassy feet between them.

She curbed the immediate impulse to fly into his arms and wrap hers tightly around his neck in exuberant relief, as she'd done at his arrival to the farm three years before, during his last visit home.

Something wasn't right.

He moved closer to the porch edge, while all the time she felt as if she were living in a bizarre dream. He stared straight at her but didn't seem to know her. Had she changed so much? She'd grown taller, her body more curvaceous and womanly, her hair almost auburn; but her face hadn't altered so greatly that he should look at her as if she were a complete stranger. He appeared similar to the last photograph she'd seen, though his unkempt hair had grown roguishly long, to brush the tops of his shoulders. And then there was that beard. She noticed he was as slim and well built as ever, with broad shoulders and a narrow waist. She pulled her brows together in concern. On deeper study he seemed too slender, as if he'd not been eating lately. . .or eating well.

That she should quietly ponder such things while her heart had awakened and was hammering cartwheels against her ribs amazed her.

"Who are you?" His body tensed as he wrapped his hand around the post, using it to step down. "Who's there. . . ? I *know* you're there. Speak up! I can hear your clothes rustle in the wind."

Her vocal chords as frozen as the rest of her, Clemmie drew in a sharp audible breath, pain crushing her heart and filming her eyes with tears. He jerked his head as if he'd heard her bare inhalation of air.

Oh, God, no. . .please no. . .don't let it be true. . . .

But the longer she watched him, the more she realized her incoherent prayer came in vain. Joel frowned, an anxious expression momentarily touching his eyes. . .his remarkable, crystalline eyes. Heavenly blue eyes that always had and still did make her heart shift in beats. Eyes that now looked straight through her. . .

Because they couldn't see her.

Her dear sweet Joel was blind.

two

How?

How had such a horrible tragedy happened to such a handsome young man who'd had everything going for him, who had once been brimming over with vitality and life? Joel was still beautiful, his features like that of a Raphaelite angel—or at least what Clemmie could see above his beard. As he slowly drew near, she could see faint lines never there before, and his skin had become a shade sallow, as though he didn't go outdoors as often as he once had.

She wanted to weep bitterly, wanted to turn on her heel and run back the way she had come, far and fast. At the same time, she wanted to run to him and hold him tightly in a strange mix of relief and despair. But she knew he would scorn any show of pity. So she stood, silent and dumb as a scarecrow, while he continued to draw closer.

"Why won't you speak?" he snapped. "You never see a blind man before?" He snorted in impatience. "You can't pretend you're not there. I'm not fooled by your silence, even if my eyes can be."

His voice lacked any real emotion, except to snap with sarcasm. This was a Joel she didn't know. His surliness both unnerved and saddened her.

He took in a long, deep breath through his nostrils. "I can smell your scent. Thea doesn't grow lilacs. I know you're there—so speak up, confound you!"

He came to a stop, only a foot away. She couldn't take her eyes off his flawless features, his beautiful, clear, useless eyes. She brushed away the tears that dripped down her cheeks.

"Loretta left the house while Thea was on the phone—" She blundered the reply, barely aware of what she said. Her voice had grown huskier over the years, was hoarse now, and she suddenly felt grateful he wouldn't recognize it. "I didn't think she should be left unattended."

"Yes, I hear her giggling. And that darn cat yowling. But that doesn't explain why *you're* here."

"I'm—I'm an acquaintance of Thea's." Clemmie wasn't sure why she gave that explanation, so she rambled aimlessly on. "I came to—to see about. . ." She stopped, realizing she couldn't air her key reason for her visit—to discover if Herbert or Thea knew of Joel's whereabouts. Clearly they did.

"To see about. . .a job as a nanny?" he filled in when she didn't continue, his manner curt. "Or maybe you're a curiosity seeker from the neighborhood, eager to learn what terrible secret Thea's been hiding in her backyard?" With that flair Joel still possessed, he swept his hand before his person from collarbone to thigh. "So, had your fill of gawking yet?"

The sudden slam of the kitchen door alerted Clemmie to Thea's presence. A rapid glance showed the woman hurrying their way, alarm in her eyes. Clemmie forestalled her before she could speak, her mind instantly jumping into gear.

"I'm not any such thing. My name's Marielle." She gave her middle name before Thea could introduce them. She sensed Thea gape at her. "I've come for a visit. I didn't mean to intrude."

"That's *exactly* what you're doing." Joel didn't curb his caustic words. "Now if you'll excuse me, I'm done providing entertainment for the day." He whipped around before she could respond and stomped back to the porch as though he'd trod the course often and had it memorized.

He entered the shed-like building. The slam of the door shot through the air like the report of a shotgun. Neither woman spoke. At last Clemmie looked at Thea, who appeared almost remorseful.

"We need to talk," she said quietly, and Thea nodded, leading the way back to the kitchen.

Clemmie sat down at the table, feeling like an invisible

puppeteer must have control of her limbs; she didn't understand how she could be moving them. She stared into the cup of coffee Thea set before her, not even thinking to add her usual lump of sugar. Right now she needed it black. Black and strong.

She took a sip, wincing as the liquid scalded her tongue. A thousand questions flew through her mind, and she grabbed one at random. "I'm assuming he lives here?"

"Yes."

"How long?"

Thea exhaled deeply. "He didn't want anyone to know."

"That's obvious. But now I do. So you no longer have any reason to conceal such information."

Thea reluctantly nodded. "Herbert found him over a year ago."

"Found him?"

"In a hospital. He'd been searching. Joel usually kept contact, but then all correspondence abruptly ended. The reporter in Herbert investigated and found him."

Clemmie wasn't sure she wanted to hear the rest, but she needed to know.

"How did it happen?"

"He was better than you see him now, when Herbert found him. Well, physically, that is. Emotionally he was a wreck, much like he is today. Only he's grown more bitter. At first Joel took a job with Herbert at the newspaper. Shortly after that he started complaining of headaches and began losing his vision a little at a time. One day he couldn't see at all."

"But *how?*"

"An accident. He'd been out of the navy for a while. From what I understand, he was with friends when it happened. One of them was driving and lost control. The driver was killed, and Joel was badly hurt—thrown from the car. Strangely there were no signs of blindness then. It took about a month. I don't remember the medical reasons Herbert gave, but Joel's been walking around like half a man ever since. Hiding here. Becoming a recluse. We tried to get him to move in with us, into the house, but he refused. Herbert almost had to twist his arm to get him to accept our help—and you know what best friends those two have always been. We finally convinced him to stay, but he was resolute about keeping his distance. He insisted on living in the shed, and Herbert finally agreed, making the necessary adjustments. It was the only way he could keep an eye on Joel. Herbert has been very concerned about him; we both have."

Each stabbing word inflicted a wound in Clemmie's heart. Now she understood why he'd made no contact, and that hurt almost as much.

"He wouldn't even contact my parents to tell them?"

"He didn't want handouts."

"*Handouts?*" Upset, Clemmie repeated the word forcefully.

Thea lightly grazed her teeth along her lip, as if uncertain she should answer.

"There's more, isn't there? Please, tell me."

Thea searched her face then nodded. "There's an operation that could relieve the pressure of whatever is pushing against his optic nerve, but it costs a great deal of money."

When she paused, Clemmie filled in the rest, her anger at Joel's mule-headedness rising to the fore. "So he decided it was better to stay blind than to tell my parents what happened and ask for a loan? The fool man," she muttered under her breath.

"I take care of him as much as I'm able," Thea continued. "Doing his laundry, straightening up after him, bringing him meals. That sort of thing."

"It must be difficult, taking care of your family and your home, too."

Thea glanced into her coffee, her solemn expression making it clear.

"Let me help."

"What?" Thea's head jerked up in shock.

"I can do all those things. I have some free time on my hands, and that would give you a needed break."

Thea smiled, uncertain. "You're kind to offer."

"Nothing kind about it. Actually I'm selfish. Joel needs someone not just to tidy up after him and feed him, but to... be there." She had difficulty explaining her feelings when even she didn't understand them. "I want to do whatever I can to help him."

"He's changed, Clemmie."

"We've all changed."

"No, you don't understand." Thea fidgeted. "He's...different. Hard. Angry at the world. At God most of all."

The news didn't surprise Clemmie, though it did distress her.

"He takes it out on anyone within reach of his voice. He can be cruel."

"Violent?" Clemmie whispered in dismay. "He hasn't struck you?" Joel often had been the mastermind behind pranks at the refuge when he was a boy, but she'd never known him to initiate physical violence. At least not that she remembered.

"No no. It's just that he's so...caustic. With his words."

Clemmie exhaled in relief. "If you're worried about me—don't be. I'm not afraid of anything Joel might dish out. I really want to do this."

"Don't you think he'll feel threatened and angry when you tell him who you are? That someone from his past has learned the truth of the misfortune he's tried so hard to hide?"

"You're right." Clemmie heaved a sigh. "Knowing him—at least based on what I once knew of him—he'd be furious."

"He hasn't changed in that regard."

Clemmie frowned, again not surprised. His foolish pride had prevented him from contacting those who loved him, who would have cared for him. After hearing Joel's story from Thea, Clemmie knew him well enough to be certain that if she were to reveal her identity, it would end her plan to help him.

"And he won't be mad at just you. He'll blame Herbert and me as well."

"All right. So. . ." Clemmie carelessly shrugged one shoulder. "We won't tell him."

"What?" Thea looked at her as if she'd suggested they take a torch to his walls and burn down his home. "You can't be serious."

"Marielle *is* my middle name. He'd never remember that, even if he did once know it. Which I doubt anyone told him. Mama wasn't in the habit of speaking it. Only when she was really upset with me. And if Joel ever did overhear, I highly doubt he would connect the two. Not like he would if I introduced myself as Clemmie."

"Tell me you're not actually going to pretend to be someone else."

"Only for a little while. Just until Joel feels comfortable having me around. I'll tell him eventually."

Thea frowned in disapproval. "I don't know. . . ."

"You said your hands are full. This will give you extra time to take care of your family. I'll take full blame should he find out. But there's no reason he should. I've changed over the last three years, my voice included. I was little more than a child when he last saw me."

Now that the shock of finding him—and in such a tragic state—had partially worn off, Clemmie wasn't sure why it felt so important to try to reconnect with Joel again. But at least this way she could share in his life without being considered the intrusion he might think her if he knew the truth.

She was pathetic.

She was walking a thin line, and she knew it.

But this was Joel. Not some stranger. And he was in clear need of help, help she was only too willing to give.

"I'll talk it over with Herbert tonight," Thea said at last. "I can't give my consent without him knowing the facts."

"Fair enough. Ring me at Hannah's when you reach a decision."

Whatever the two decided, Clemmie grew firm in her resolve to remain in Joel's life, somehow. Now that she'd found him, she wasn't about to lose him again.

three

The air blew cold, moist. It would rain. Again. The skies for him were always dark, but so was the earth and everything in it. Only in strong sunlight could Joel discern vague shadows—all of them a darker shade of gray than the black that continually filled his world.

Day.

Night.

It was all the same to him. The same void, the same darkness.

All that was left of his life.

With a grimace he stepped out onto the porch and wondered for the umpteenth time why he bothered. Why leave his four walls to visit the outdoors when he couldn't see the grass or the skies or the hydrangea bushes that rimmed Herbert's home? Where his eyes failed him, his other senses had sharpened, and before he found his way to his chair, he picked up an aroma different from the fresh soil near his porch that Loretta had dug up in her play or the clean scent of rain coating the air.

The scent of lilacs.

He scowled, crossing his arms over his chest, and turned toward the whisper of footsteps he heard over the breeze.

"You again. What do you want this time? Didn't get enough entertainment ogling the blind man the other day?"

"How did you know...?"

Her voice, quiet and lovely with a throaty huskiness, trailed off in shocked confusion.

His lips curled into a hard smile. "I told you. I may be blind, but I'm no fool."

"I never said you were. But I could have been anyone. How

did you know it was me?"

He decided not to answer. "You haven't stated your business for coming here again. Does the term *trespassing* mean nothing to you?"

"My business?" A hint of amusement laced her tone. "I suppose you could call it that. But for your information, I'm hardly trespassing."

He didn't like this sudden turn, as if she had the upper hand. It made him feel even more vulnerable and at a loss than he already was. To bring things back to his control, he relied on his acerbic behavior. His jaw hardened.

"State it, then beat it. I don't want you here."

"Well, Joel, that's just too bad. Because here is where I'll be staying."

Her casual use of his name and stubborn response threw him for a moment.

"That's 'Mr. Litton' to you. And no, you're not. Not anywhere near here. Go back to the house and visit Thea, since you're her friend. Or if you'd like, I could bodily remove you from these premises."

Silence answered, and he could tell he'd addled her. He smirked in his victory, small though it was.

"Very well, Mr. Litton. If you prefer such a silly formality in title, so be it. There's no need to be so rude. And you may call me Marielle."

Irate, he unclasped his folded arms and took a swift step toward her. "I won't call you anything! Except gone from my home. Now! Scram!"

"My, we did wake up in a grumpy mood this morning, didn't we?"

Joel blinked with shock at her wry words and heard her approach. He took an involuntary step back. The thud of her steps hit the planking, the smell of lilacs assaulting him. He felt the air stir as she breezed past—then heard the door he'd left ajar swing fully open.

"Whatta ya think you're doing?" he demanded, moving her

way. He just prevented himself from following through with his threat of reaching out to find and grab her arm and throw her off his porch. "Don't you know a direct order to go when you hear one? I haven't given you any invitation to invade my privacy."

"Oh, I'm sorry. Didn't Thea tell you?" Her tone shifted from utter brashness to mild chagrin. "I'm your new housekeeper and cook."

"My *what*?" The breath escaped his lungs as if he'd been punched in the stomach.

"I'm going to take care of you."

Over his dead body! Her words rankled, stiffening his pride. "I don't need anyone looking after—"

"Thea looks after you."

"Yes, but it's her place to—" To what? Wait on him hand and foot? It wasn't her place. But this irritating woman's logic stymied him, and his words came out jumbled. "What I mean to say is, it's her home."

"And I offered to help. She's looking a bit peaked, and I thought it would ease her workload, since I have plenty of time on my hands."

The news that Thea wasn't well concerned him, though he didn't show it. Was taking care of him as well as her family such a trial? It must be. He certainly hadn't made her task any easier. Before he had time to think up a reply, he heard the woman intruder's footsteps move away and realized she'd entered his home.

Grimacing, he followed but remained on the threshold.

"This isn't necessary."

"I think it's very necessary. *Tsk,* you quite obviously need help keeping order around this place."

"Maybe I like it sloppy. It's not like I can see to know the difference."

"Well, I can. And it's just not healthy to live in such disorder."

"Put those down!"

She gave a shocked gasp at the same time he heard the

buckles of his suspenders hit the planks and the rumple of his slacks follow. It unnerved him for her to touch his personal items.

"H—how did you know I was holding anything?"

"I have very acute hearing. There's nothing you can get by me."

"I wasn't trying to." She released a tired little sigh. "Look, can we at least try to give this a go?"

"I didn't ask you to come here or invite you inside. You're not here by mutual agreement." Remembering what she'd said about Thea being exhausted, he gave in with a grumble. "Trial basis. One day. If I'm not happy with your work here, you promise to leave and never come back."

"One week. And if you're pleased with my work, you agree to keep me on the rest of the summer."

He smiled wide, showing his teeth, sure he'd found the winning hand. The clinks of the dishes and silver she was gathering abruptly stilled, and all went silent, except for her slightest indrawn breath. He wondered what had happened; apparently something had occurred to make her react with such shock. Had she seen a mouse? He'd heard the rodents scuttling over the floor at night when he couldn't sleep.

"I can't pay you." He tossed his trump card at her. "Not one red cent. I haven't got the money."

"Th—that's all right. I don't need wages."

Irritated that she'd pulled an ace from her sleeve, he scowled. "Ridiculous! What kind of woman are you that you'd want a job and not get paid for it? Especially in these hard times."

"I only want to help," she practically whispered.

"I don't need your pity!"

"I'm not giving it. I mean I want to help Thea."

He couldn't argue with that logic, which made him all the more disgusted. "I still don't like the idea. And I don't take charity."

"All right. How about this: I'll think up a way you can pay me back."

He scoffed a laugh. "Sorry, not able to do much manual labor these days."

"Doesn't matter. I'll think up something you can do for me, if you're so insistent not to let me volunteer. Something to which you'll be agreeable and which won't make you feel you're taking charity. Is it a deal?"

He thought her proposition over, wondering what she might come up with as substitute payment. He probably wouldn't have to worry; he doubted she would last two days.

"Okay, one week. First rule: hands off my private things. Second rule: Leave me alone. Got it?"

"Yes."

"Swell." With nothing more to say, Joel walked back outside.

His shed had never felt so confining.

da

Clemmie blew out a long breath, as if she'd just escaped being the unwitting target of a firing squad or, better to describe her situation, fought hand-to-hand combat with cutting vocabulary. His tongue was as sharp as Thea had warned, but Clemmie had been raised at the refuge and had learned to spar with words while growing up among young scalawags or risk getting sliced to smithereens. Joel would find himself matched to a worthy opponent.

She chuckled at how her mind compared their conversation to battle. And in this, their first skirmish, she had come out the victor.

"Be prepared, Joel Litton," she whispered, looking at the door he'd left ajar. "You've met your match this day. I'm not about to let you wallow in that pit of self-despair you've dug for yourself. Clemmie Lyons has come to town."

She smiled at her private declaration.

Just like Christian in her favorite allegory, Clemmie felt like a pilgrim about to embark on a journey. A masked pilgrim, in withholding her identity, which made her goal to get through to Joel trickier, but as Darcy always said, "Where there's a river too wide, somewhere there's bound to be a bridge, and if not, it's up to you to make one." She'd proven that when a person's will was strong, success ultimately followed. What Uncle Brent coined as her "harebrained schemes" always worked out in the end. So why couldn't Clemmie do the same and cross her own devised bridge to reach Joel?

She set down the cleaning tools she'd brought and planted her hands on her hips. In the dim light from the doorway she took quick inventory of what still looked very much like a shed. Next time she would need to bring a lantern to see well.

The area was less than half the size of the bedroom she'd been given at Hannah's. A single cot sat in the corner, a table and chair stood at the foot, and an old-fashioned, big-bellied, small cookstove took up the opposite corner, most likely to provide heat in winter. Two shelves were mounted to a wall. They bore odd and sundry items, including one single place setting of dishes and silverware. There were no windows, and ugly dark siding of some coarse nature covered the walls. She assumed it was put there to insulate the room in colder months. Not one decorative embellishment cheered the place, not a picture, not a colorful rug, not even a small memento.

Not that Joel would be able to see them if they were there.

Her vision swam, the room going wavy as her eyes watered. The first night she had returned to Hannah's, she'd enclosed herself in her room and thrown herself across the bed, bawling like a baby over Joel's tragic circumstances.

Not this time.

She pulled her lips in a thin line. She *would not* pity him. Joel could have chosen to have that operation, to call her parents and get a loan, though she knew they would never ask for recompense, but his stubborn pride had gotten in the way. Infuriating! Nor could she bring up the subject without revealing her identity, and that would guarantee he'd throw her bodily from his home and slam the door in her face. No questions asked; no explanations allowed.

"Drat it all!" She whisked the dish towel with unnecessary force along the table she'd cleared, scattering a shower of crumbs to the floor.

Her endeavor to help would most likely try her patience to a worn frazzle, but as she'd told Herbert on the phone when he finally rang Hannah's two nights after her initial visit, she not only wanted to do this for Joel, she needed to. As a youngster he had championed her when he didn't tease, and she wished to return the favor of being a friend to him.

The thought of not seeing Joel again was unacceptable. After she rang off with Herbert, she emphatically assured a concerned Hannah that she was long over her schoolgirl infatuation. Hannah had been sympathetic and encouraging, relieved after hearing Clemmie's plan, since she had her hands full for the next month helping her mother prepare things for the bazaar.

"Maybe God had a hand in this all along," her friend had surmised, sounding much like her wise mother, before she had giggled like the fifteen-year-old she was. "Well, of course He did. Silly me. He always does have a plan, doesn't He?"

Clemmie glumly reminded herself of that nugget of encouragement as she fetched the broom she'd brought and took out her frustrations with vicious swipes along the boards.

One thing could be said about trapped irritation—it made cleaning go by a great deal faster.

With her work done, she gathered her supplies and walked outdoors. Joel sat rigid in his chair, in profile to her and facing the woods. The small orange tabby of the other day wove a loving arc around his ankles. Joel didn't acknowledge Clemmie's presence, but she did see him flinch the moment she walked out the door.

"I did what I could," she began, "but that floor could use a good scrubbing. I'll bring the items tomorrow and do it then."

"That's not necessary."

She ignored his curt response.

"Also, just so you know it, I took your clothes to be laundered."

His hand gripped his knees hard, his knuckles whitening.

"I told you not to touch my personal things."

"Unless you plan on becoming a poster child for 'bum of the century,' I found that gathering your soiled laundry was even more essential than cleaning the floors, which, by the way, are also darkly spotted. Now, if you'll excuse me, I'll be seeing to your lunch."

He clenched his lips into a white line, as if withholding another negative response. But he couldn't very well tell her not to cook him a meal since he had to eat or starve to death. Eyeing his lean frame, she wondered if he had tried doing that.

Biting off words she knew would not be appreciated, she marched off his porch and crossed the yard to Thea's. Inside the cheery yellow kitchen Clemmie let her facade drop—not that Joel could have seen her distress in any case, but he sensed things so strongly he might have felt it.

"Things not go so well, I take it?" Thea greeted, glancing at her and tapping the spoon against a bowl she used to mix batter.

"I wasn't expecting it to." Clemmie set the cleaning basket on the floor with a sigh. "And I received my full expectation."

Thea tsked and went back to her chore.

"I appreciate you letting me use your things."

Thea waved aside her thanks. "I'd never expect you to bring your own supplies on your walk here every afternoon. Just leave them there. I'll put them away."

"I'd like to help with the meals. I feel bad about infringing on your generosity."

"Are you kidding?" Thea looked at her in shock. "You've been such a big help to me! The least I can do is to provide you with lunch every day. I've cooked for all of us for so long I don't mind. It's become a habit. Hope you don't mind pancakes?" Thea looked up from dropping a dollop of batter onto the hot pan.

"I've never had them for anything but breakfast, but I do like them. And I wouldn't mind contributing in the kitchen some days. I'm a very good cook, and that's not bragging. Darcy taught me everything I know."

"High praise indeed!" Thea smiled. "In that case I'll take you up on your offer. And that makes me think of something." Her expression became contrite. "I'm sorry our car isn't in working order for Herbert to give you a lift home. It's a blessing his job is only a fifteen-minute walk from here and that he's kept it. So many are out of work right now. But I guess where there is life, there is always news, and the public wants to stay informed."

Clemmie had to smile. As a boy at the refuge, Herbert sometimes squealed on his pals and got them in trouble. She was glad his tendency to broadcast events had matured to an acceptable position as a reporter for *The Cedarbrook Herald*. Joel had been the ringleader of the close-knit bunch of boys, his chums always looking to him for answers. Now he'd closed himself off from the entire world, except from his best buddy, Herbert.

"At least Joel turned to someone," she aired her thoughts aloud, only just realizing they had nothing to do with the present conversation.

Thea looked at her closely. "Hmm." She flipped a pancake. "Well, Herbert gave him no choice. Once Joel lost his sight, he was a fish out of water and had to rely heavily on Herbert, hating every second of it." She shook her head. "Men and their pride. I understand that during their childhood, Herbert had his eyes bandaged for weeks after Joel got whitewash in them during one of their spats. The two forgave each other, and Herbert then relied on Joel. That's the sole reason Joel agreed to let us help him, I think. Herbert brought the incident up and told him he wanted to pay him back—even though Joel was the one who painted Herbert's face with the whitewash."

Clemmie hadn't yet been born during that time, though over the years she'd heard about the alarming results of Darcy's first whitewash contest.

At the sound of the front door opening, both women turned their heads.

"Thea? I'm home."

Her face bright with pleasure, Thea set down the spoon and hurried to greet her husband. Soon she returned, Herbert behind her.

"Well now, aren't you a sight for sore eyes? You're quite the grown-up lady!" He held out his arms to Clemmie, and she grinned as they exchanged hugs. Clemmie stepped back to do her own survey. Still of medium height and build, still a little on the stout side, his hair the same shade of russet, Herbert was easily recognizable.

"I see you haven't changed," Clemmie returned.

"Oh, I wouldn't say that. We've all changed. But look at you! Last I saw, you were just a squirt with bright orange braids."

"Hmph." She crossed her arms. "Not that bright."

"Should you two be talking so loudly?" Thea interrupted with a glance toward the open kitchen window.

"It wouldn't matter." Herbert shook his head. "He rarely steps foot off that porch, and we're not exactly shouting for our words to carry that far. How's he doing today?"

"The same."

Herbert and Thea exchanged a long, telling look. Clemmie didn't add her own opinion of Joel's irascible behavior. Herbert looked at her.

"Are you sure you want to do this? It's not too late to back out."

"Yes. And no, I don't want to back out."

She didn't hesitate with her answer, and Herbert chuckled wryly. "I should have known you'd say that. I'm still not comfortable with the idea of keeping the truth of who you are from him though."

"If I tell him, I'll never get through to him." She unwittingly aired her core reason for going through with her ruse.

He peered at her sharply, making her want to squirm. "Tell me again that you're over your girlhood infatuation, that this desire to help is all in friendship."

"It is." She laughed. "Like you said, we've all grown up and changed, Herbert. I know the way I used to behave was quite silly. I'm beyond that."

"Good." He gave a pleased nod. "I wouldn't want you hurt. And, Clemmie, keeping the truth from him could wind up putting you in quite a pickle."

She smiled upon hearing the echo of Darcy's admonishments when doling out advice to wayward young hooligans. It was amazing how, no matter their differences, children picked up sayings from the adults by whom they'd been taught. She even found herself speaking some of Uncle Brent's professorial words now and then.

"I promise I'll tell him. When the time is right."

Herbert twisted his mouth in uncertainty, mulling over the prospect. "Well, nothing else has worked. If you really think you can reach him, then you have my support. But I have to warn you, Clemmie—"

"You'd better start calling me by my middle name—Marielle."

He sighed. "Once Joel finds out, he's not going to be one bit happy to learn he was hoodwinked."

"That's why he can't find out. Not until I tell him."

Clemmie didn't want to think about that disturbing day to come.

four

"If you've come to offer advice, Herbert, you can just stop right there, turn around, and go back the way you came."

The rustling in the grass reached a sudden halt.

"How'd you know..."

"That it was you?" Joel laughed bitterly at the surprise in Herbert's voice. "That you should even need to ask such a question by now baffles me. I smelled you."

"I took a bath."

Joel grunted in disdain. "Good to know."

"Unlike some people I could mention."

"The odor of ink from the printing press gives you away. It sticks to your clothes."

"Are you planning to adopt the Bohemian look, ole pal? You could do with a haircut, too. And a shave."

"And your steps are faster. Brisker than the women's."

"Ah, the women. Speaking of, how's the new girl working out for you? I'll bet she'd give you a shave if you asked."

"There's also a trace of odor from those cheap cigars your boss smokes. It seeps into your clothes, and all of it carries to me on the breeze."

"Are we going to dance around this subject all night?"

"Is that a question that requires an answer?"

Herbert snorted in exasperation. "The new girl. Marielle. What do you think of her?"

Joel fidgeted, uneasy to be put on the spot. "She annoys me."

Annoy wasn't exactly the word to describe the emotion he felt with regard to the woman. His notice of her fell somewhere between irritation and intrigue. He hadn't been able to get her out of his mind since she stepped foot on the property a few days before and challenged him. Now that she worked for him and they had shared in more lengthy conversations than Joel's usual—"Get out!"—something about her niggled at the back of his mind. He couldn't put his finger on what it was, which put him in an even grouchier mood, since feeling clueless about a situation made him feel more vulnerable.

It was bad enough he'd lost his sight. He wouldn't let her scramble his mind.

"Not thinking happy thoughts, I take it." Herbert's referral to his daughter's trite saying carried an undercurrent of amusement and triggered Joel's defensive response.

"Tell me just what I have to be happy about? That the sun never gets in my eyes? That I'm spared having to stare at my drab walls? Or that I don't have to see your ugly mug every day?" He shifted in his chair in mock deliberation. "Come to think of it, that is cause for celebration."

"You can be happy you have a roof over your head and three meals a day. Entire families are starving, what with the state of things in our nation. You aren't the only one suffering."

"Spare me the lectures."

"Don't worry. I won't bother. It's useless anyway. All you can think about is yourself."

Joel clutched his hands around his thighs, rubbing them to his knees in aggravated silence. Uncomfortable to have his behavior criticized, whether he deserved it or not, he offered no reply. His old friend had been nothing but helpful, offering him room and board, and Joel was helpless to repay him. That stung worse than anything—having to be a useless sponge that soaked up others' generosity. Finding work these days for a sighted man was near impossible; for a blind man it was laughable. He hated being dependent on others and often found himself taking out his frustrations on the ones who made him feel that way.

"It's been over a year, and you still act as if it were yesterday," Herbert said.

"I wonder if you'd be half as glib if the roles were switched,"

Joel shot back darkly. "It's easy to tell me how to behave when you're not the one who was once living life, happy as a clam, and in the blink of an eye—pardon the expression—had everything ripped away from him."

"You haven't lost everything," Herbert responded with weary patience.

"I might as well have! I can't do anything but sit here day after lousy, stinking day—and for what? Why did I survive? Tell me! Did God decide I needed some special punishment because things were going so right for me during that all-too-brief period in my life?"

"Right for you? You were out of a job before the accident."

"So is at least a quarter of the nation as you pointed out. But at least I was a whole man before I got struck down from on high."

"God's not like that. You know it."

"No I don't. Didn't Saul get struck blind on the road to Damascus?"

"I'm surprised you remember anything from our studies at the refuge."

Joel scoffed, but Herbert continued. "Anyway, that was different. It was temporary and for a reason. If you remember, Jesus healed the blind. He didn't make them that way."

"Well, He did a fine job with me! But you're right. I'm being punished for thinking only of myself. I deserve this."

Herbert blew out an exasperated sigh. "I didn't mean any such thing, and I'm not going to stand here and listen to you wallow in self-pity. It's a handicap, Joel. Not the end of the world. Learn to make the most of it, since you chose to live with it. It's about time you did."

"It's so easy for you, isn't it?" Joel's voice was deceptively polite. "Doling out advice like you've actually lived through the situation."

"I have."

"Not the same. You got your sight back."

"But at the time I didn't know if I ever would."

"And as I recall, you were a titanic pest, ordering everyone at the refuge to wait on you hand and foot and manipulating Darcy into reading all of that blasted pirate book to you in under a week's time."

Herbert chuckled. "True. But the fact remains, I know what it's like to suddenly be without sight and have to rely on others for just about everything. I know what you're going through."

"You were eleven when it happened. You had no life."

"You think age has anything to do with feeling scared or helpless?"

Joel gripped his knees more tightly, not wanting to continue with the conversation. "Tell Thea to find someone else."

"What?"

"That girl—Marilou. I have a sneaking suspicion she won't work out."

"Her name's Marielle. And you promised her a week's trial."

"She told you?" Joel groused, wondering if the woman was trying to manipulate Herbert behind Joel's back in order to keep her position.

"Just why don't you think she'll work out? She seems efficient, skilled, willing to do whatever is asked. Just the type of help you need."

"She's too bossy, too nosy, and speaks her mind without being asked."

"Like I said," Herbert drawled. "Just what you need."

Joel didn't miss the laughter in Herbert's voice.

"And speaking of the wise lady, she's headed this way."

Joel straightened his back in irritation. Following Herbert's lighthearted declaration, he heard the whisper of footsteps rustle across the yard, steadily growing louder, accompanied by the rich scent of meat loaf and potatoes.

"Hello." Her voice came cheery. "I brought supper."

"I'm not hungry," Joel replied petulantly, angry at his stomach for its eager lurch at the aroma of delicious food.

"Well, that's just too bad, because you're going to eat."

"No. I'm not." His reply came just as obstinate.

"Yes. You are. I just spent the past two hours helping Thea and slaving over a hot stove, and you most certainly will eat every morsel I brought you, Mr. Joel Litton."

Before he could counter her verbal attack, he heard her swift footsteps march with determination inside his house. He turned to where Herbert quietly chuckled.

"You see what I mean? She's impossible! There's no way I'm putting up with her insolence for one solid week."

"What I think I see is Thea at the window. Yup, there she is. It's my suppertime, too. And that meat loaf smells absolutely scrumptious."

"You're going to just go and leave things like they are?"

"Leave things like what?"

"Her," he growled between clenched teeth. "This situation. I was hoping you might side with me in getting her to leave me alone for good and go back to wherever it is she came from."

"Aren't you the one always telling me you can do fine on your own and don't need any mollycoddling? After all, you're bigger than she is. And she's a girl."

"Aw, go chase yourself," Joel snapped, in no mood to put up with his tormentor's jests.

"I'll drop by after supper."

"Don't bother."

Joel grimaced when his so-called friend laughed again as he headed for his house.

"Mr. Litton?" came his new tormentor's voice from inside.

Crossing his arms over his chest, Joel determined to ignore her presence and never give in to the intrusive dame.

❧

Clemmie threw open the door to her room and flung her purse on the bed.

"Imbecile!"

Her hat followed.

"Ignoramus!"

She ripped apart the buttons of her cardigan and tore it from one side, flinging her arm and flapping it around to rid herself of the rest of her sweater. "Mule-headed...pigheaded... dimwitted...obstinate!" She muttered each insult with each flap of her arm. Her cardigan at last gave way and with one final wave shot to the bed.

"I didn't know you could be a mule and a pig at the same time." Hannah's amused voice came from the doorway.

Clemmie swung around to face her. "When your name is Joel Litton, you can! He is such a, such a..." She sought for appropriate words.

"Cantankerous idiot?"

"Exactly!"

Clemmie whirled around again, falling to a sitting position on the bed. She crossed her arms over her chest, feeling as if she could spit nails.

"So I take it working for the 'master of mischief' wasn't smooth sailing today?"

"Ha!" Clemmie grunted the exclamation in disdain. "Not only would he *not* eat the perfectly lovely meal I brought him at the end of the day, but he threw the plate at the wall when I insisted he eat it, and he missed me by bare inches!"

"He didn't!" Hannah's eyes grew wide as she drew closer. She worked not to smile.

"He did. And it's not funny, Hannah. They eat meat only twice a week. And just look at my skirt." She groaned, lifting the brown cotton splotched with smears from the flying mashed potatoes and gravy.

"It'll wash."

"Oh, I know that." Clemmie sighed, thinking of the hardened food she would have to scrub from the wall, baseboards, and floor tomorrow. Joel had cursed her, ordering her out and yelling the directive in cruel, shocking words that she would never tell Hannah, much less say aloud to anyone, and she hadn't dared stay longer and clean up the mess.

"Are you going back?"

"Of course."

At Clemmie's emphatic and quick reply, Hannah couldn't

hold back the laughter any longer. She wrapped her arms around herself, her enthusiasm growing as she toppled to her side on the counterpane.

"Stop it. It's not funny." Clemmie felt her lips turn up at the corners. "Stop it, I said, or you're likely to cast a kitten!" Her smile grew.

Hannah's glee became infectious, and Clemmie was soon laughing as well, the two girls holding each other until they got a grip on sobriety again.

"He can be a terror and a trial," Clemmie mused once she'd calmed. "I can't say I wasn't warned. But I'm no quitter."

"I admire that about you. Me, I often give up too easily or worry what other people might say or think."

"Well, I'm not worried about that, either."

"Except when it comes to Joel finding out who you are."

The girls grew quiet.

"Do you also think I'm wrong to keep it from him?" Clemmie eyed her friend. She had earlier told her that Thea shared such reservations, and so, apparently, did Herbert. "I'm only keeping quiet for his own good. If he knew who I was at this rocky moment in our all-too-brief association, anything positive I want to accomplish would be lost, and he'd remain in his pathetic little pit of despair forever."

Hannah grinned. "Like *Pilgrim's Progress*. I read that for a book report."

"Exactly."

Hannah lowered her gaze, growing introspective. "I'm not exactly sure Mama would agree with your methods. She would say deceit is deceit, plain and simple, but your heart's in the right place, I think." She peered intently at Clemmie as if she could see through her. "What do you hope to gain by all this? You're not still all gaga over him, are you?"

"Of course not. I told you. I'm not a child any longer."

"I know that, silly. But, well, you're a woman. And he's a man."

Her words brought the strangest tingle to Clemmie's skin.

"I only want to help him. That is, if he'd put his armor and weapons down long enough to let me."

"Weapons?"

"The tongue can be a powerful weapon."

"Oh, right."

"And his throwing arm isn't half-bad either."

They both giggled.

"Well, like I told you when you first brought it up, I'll support you however I can. With this bazaar Mother's partly in charge of, I find my days occupied. I'm just glad you found something to do—but still sorry I'm not here much of the day."

"It's not as if we don't spend any time together. We're talking now."

"That's true." Hannah's smile again brightened. "So, what's your first plan of attack in 'Operation Save Joel'?"

" 'Operation Save Joel'—I like that! I do often feel as if I'm in a war zone when I'm around him." Clemmie dropped her chin to her hand, deep in thought. Suddenly she smiled.

"Is that offer to help immediately available?"

"Sure. What do you have in mind?"

"I need you to take me to your grocer's. I have money from what Grandfather gave me. And both Father and Uncle Brent slipped me some, all without any of them knowing." She laughed with affection at the antics of her male relatives, each of whom had tried to evade notice when giving her "a little cash" before she left for the train. "Aunt Darcy always said the way to a man's heart is through his stomach, though what I really want is to get through to his brain. But maybe that's the best route to get there."

"Are you sure just a small, teensy part of you wouldn't like to get through to his heart as well?" Hannah teased, holding her thumb and forefinger a slight distance apart. "Are you absolutely sure you're as immune to him as you say?"

Hannah's eyes were much too sharp. Mumbling an offhand "Of course," Clemmie rose from the bed and shrugged back into her sweater.

The bitter, cantankerous Joel she now contended with was far removed from the easygoing boy and pleasant young man she once knew. Strangely, however, that didn't deflect her desire to keep him in her life. She didn't elaborate on her feelings to Hannah, not wanting to admit there might be more than a grain of truth to her statement.

She was beyond schoolgirl obsessions, for pity's sake. But then, she was no longer a schoolgirl, as Hannah had pointed out. She was a woman. And blind or not, Joel was every bit as much a man as before, the same man who could still make her heart beat triple time or come to a sudden, breathtaking stop.

When he wasn't being impossible.

"To the grocer's then?" Clemmie asked cheerily, tamping down any spiraling thoughts that might resurrect the old dream.

"This late?"

"If they're still open, I'd like to get an early start tomorrow and do a few things while your uncle's cook isn't in the kitchen. Think she'll mind me using it?"

"Annie? No, she's gone home to her family for the night. And Mr. Carter does keep late hours on weekends, hoping for more business. So his shop would be open, I would think."

"Perfect."

"I'll ask Father to drive us."

"It's too far to walk?"

"Unlike you, I don't walk." Hannah gave a little shiver. "Not when there are four perfectly good wheels and an engine begging to be used."

Clemmie giggled at the silliness of her pampered friend, feeling ten times better than when she had arrived that evening. She just hoped the feeling would last through tomorrow, when she faced the temperamental lion in his confined den once again.

five

Joel sat on his porch chair, the warmth of the sun acting as a rebel to his belligerent mood. He waited for the inevitable footsteps in the grass. When they finally came, he sat so rigid they could have made a springboard to a pool out of him.

"Good morning. I brought back your clean laundry."

He grunted in reply.

"Is there anywhere special you keep it?"

"In the latrine," he bit out.

"Fine, if you're going to be that way about it." Her voice maintained a calm cheeriness, rasping against his nerves like a cheese grater. "I'll find a place to put these myself then."

Her light steps disappeared inside his shed, and with a groan he got up to follow. The last thing he wanted was her nosing through every one of his personal things.

"In that trunk," he grumbled. "At the foot of the bed."

He heard the lid creak as she raised it, the rustle of cloth as she put the articles away, and the muted thud and click as she closed the trunk.

An eternity of silence passed, though his fine-tuned ears could hear her breathing and noticed it had picked up a notch. He sensed her eyes on him.

She approached.

On involuntary impulse he backed up a step, to the porch.

Her steps halted.

His mouth thinned.

Ridiculous! He was not afraid of a girl as Herbert had implied. Especially not this girl.

With resolve Joel moved forward more than the single step back he'd taken, until he came close enough to feel the warmth of her body and to be awash in the scent of lilacs, though no part of him touched her.

She gave a sudden and soft intake of breath.

"Was there anything else?" he asked, striving to sound polite, though he would rather toss her over his shoulder and carry her from his home.

"I. . ." She gulped and swallowed loud enough for him to hear. "H–how did you. . ." He felt the stir of air as she moved past him, toward the wall. The brush of her fingertips smoothed over the oilcloth.

"I may be blind, lady, but my hands weren't amputated."

"O–of course not. I only meant. . ." She sighed. "You cleaned this?"

"No, the elves slipped in while I was asleep."

"Well, at least you never lost that charming sense of humor," she mumbled.

"What?" He grew alert at her strange choice of words and swiftly turned his head her way.

"I—that is, Herbert told me you once were quite. . .funny." Her words trailed off weakly into an explanation.

"Yeah, that's me," he quipped derisively. "Funny man Joel. Take a seat, and let me entertain you. Slapstick is my specialty. Especially if you leave my pathway cluttered."

She blew out a harsh, disgusted breath, not in the least amused, which adversely brought his first genuine smile.

"I'll just leave you to practice your act then, shall I? Though with me around, I defy you to find one thing out of place, on your floor or otherwise." To his surprised relief, he heard her retreat to the door. "I'll be back later with your supper." She hesitated, retraced her steps to the table, where he heard the silverware she scraped together, then marched out once again.

At last he was left alone. Alone, that is, except for the trace of her scent lingering in the air, surrounding him. The warm, clean smell of sunshine on skin and hair, mixed with lilacs. It stirred his traitorous thoughts into reliving the past moments.

Again that niggling sense of something not being right prickled at his mind, something he couldn't place his finger on. That, more than anything else, was what he didn't like about this new cleaning woman and cook Thea had hired. The girl unbalanced his sense of reality, setting him on an uneven keel, which made living ten times worse when all he saw was darkness.

Four more days, as he'd promised her—or rather, as she'd manipulated out of him—and then he would demand she leave. At least with the wait he couldn't be accused of not trying, as Herbert had said. Or of being intimidated by a slip of a girl.

❧

Chop!

Clemmie let loose with a cleaver, neatly slicing a potato in half. *Chop!*

Off went the head of the onion.

Chop! Chop! Chop!

The long, lean carrots became history.

"You seem to be taking more pleasure in that task than it should involve," Thea remarked in amusement as she watched her. She picked up the saucer holding a slab of creamy yellow butter. "And real butter? You're spoiling him."

Clemmie hated the butter substitute of oleo that so many people were forced to use in these hard times, what Darcy also used at the refuge. For what she had in mind, oleo wouldn't suffice, and it had been worth the extra money to procure the genuine article. She knew it would make a huge difference in flavor, too. Just this one time, and one time was all she needed for the hoped-for breakthrough.

"He needs a little spoiling. Maybe that's part of his problem." She stopped chopping long enough to cast Thea an embarrassed glance. "Oh! I didn't mean that you haven't been doing a good job of things."

Thea laughed her off. "I know. Don't worry. You're being very tolerant toward him after his ill behavior. Herbert told me," she explained at Clemmie's curious glance. "And I also know what daily interaction with Joel can entail!"

"So why do you put up with it?" Clemmie knew her own reasons, but she wondered what motivated Thea to beard the beast in his self-made cage every day.

Thea shrugged. "He's Herbert's oldest and dearest friend. Before he went blind, he really was quite the debonair fella." She sighed. "I'm also hoping that by showing him people care about what happens to him, maybe he'll draw close to God again. And that God will use me somehow to reach him. That reminder is the only thing that keeps me patient when he's in one of his moods."

"Then he really has turned from his faith?" The news distressed Clemmie.

Thea wasn't quick to answer. "He's very bitter and confused. Even before he went blind, he was getting to that point."

"Oh? But why. . ."

"He didn't actually come to Connecticut of his own free will. Did I tell you? Herbert pushed him into it, worried about the trouble Joel was getting into—or rather had gotten himself into."

"Trouble? What tr—"

A horrendous shriek followed by loud wailing cut off Clemmie's words.

"Oh dear. Loretta must have fallen. I do hope this is just a clumsy phase she's going through!" Thea hurried from the room, leaving Clemmie to deliberate her thoughts.

What had happened before his blindness to set Joel on the path of turning from God? Though she wouldn't have called him a strong Christian when he was at the refuge—not like her parents—he was no heathen. His father's long incarceration in jail had at first been the stimulus for the young Joel to become a hoodlum, but later the penalty of his father's crimes, along with the knowledge that he'd died in his cell, had made Joel want to repent and not become like the man who sired him. He'd told Clemmie on several occasions that he thought of her father as his own. So what had happened to change all that? What kind of "trouble" could Thea be referring to?

The questions revolved inside her mind. Throughout the rest of her meal preparations, she tried to come up with answers. Thea didn't return, and once all was ready, Clemmie resolved she would ask her friend at the next available opportunity. Taking a deep breath, she picked up the plate she'd prepared and a glass of water and set them on a tray.

"All right," she muttered, building up nerve. "Prepare for round two, Joel Litton, and this time I'm coming out the winner."

Loaded with her delicious weapon that with any luck would break through his barricade, she made her way to his shed. He wasn't sitting outside as she expected, and she pulled at her lip with her teeth, hesitating, before she balanced the tray with one hand and knocked.

"Get lost."

"It's me. Cl—Marielle." She caught herself just in time.

"I know who it is."

She gritted her teeth. "That knock was a courtesy, not a request. If you don't open the door to me in the next three seconds or give me a legitimate reason why I can't enter, I'm coming inside." When he didn't respond, she put her hand to the latch in resolve, her shoulder to the wood. It wouldn't budge.

He'd barricaded himself inside!

"Joel Litton, if you don't open this door right now, I'll go and get Herbert to break it down. You know me well enough by now to know I mean it!"

Silence.

"All right then, till the count of three. One. . .two. . ." Maybe she should have given him to the count of five—or perhaps ten—and wondered if it was harder for him to navigate without his vision, even in familiar areas.

"Thr—"

The barricade he'd used made a scraping sound, and the door swung open. Joel's blue eyes blazed down at her. Strange that they could see nothing, as vibrant as they were. Like living blue coals.

"What do you want?" he growled.

She tamped down a fleeting moment's nervousness. "I brought dinner."

"I'm not hungry."

"Nonsense." She managed to brush past, knocking him aside without upsetting the tray, and heard his grunt of surprise. "You have to eat. You didn't eat last night, and Thea mentioned you had no breakfast or lunch. You can't keep this up, or you'll starve to death."

"Maybe that'd be best."

She set the tray on the table with a little slam and whirled to face him. "Joel Litton, don't you dare talk that way! Shame on you! There are plenty of people suffering in this world—not just you. If everyone gave up on living, where would this nation be, I ask? We'd all be history!"

He took two steps toward her. "Don't give me any lectures, lady! You can't possibly know what it's like."

"To be blind? No. But I do know about suffering. I know what it means to hurt."

He narrowed his eyes. "What pain has a little thing like you suffered in this world? You seem disgustingly cheery most of the time."

His tense but flippant words were like blows, since he'd been the crux of much of her pain. "Oh, I've suffered. The loss of a family member. The ache of rejection. The desolation of loneliness. But I've learned to put my faith in God, even when I don't understand why those things happened. He knows all and always has an answer if I'm quiet enough to listen. Sometimes He gives no answer, just a feeling of peace."

Hardness carved his face into a mask of stone. "Don't talk to me about God! Where was God when my friend's car went over an embankment? Where was God when I had to tell his ailing mother that her only son was dead and attend his funeral and two others—but by some twist of insanity I alone survived? Where was God when his fiancée tried to overdose a week later, after learning she was pregnant with his kid?"

Shock ran cold throughout Clemmie, freezing her anger, which then melted into horrified compassion. Without thought she reached out to him. "Joel, I'm so sorry. . . ."

He knocked her hand away from his arm. "Spare me your pity. I don't need it, and I sure don't deserve it."

"Don't deserve it?"

He turned his back on her, his head lowered.

Confused by his belittling words but realizing that to extend the conversation might result in getting her thrown out a second time, she changed the subject. "Please eat. I spent a lot of time preparing this meal. I was told it's your favorite."

Joel's shoulders jerked, his stance becoming rigid again. After what seemed endless seconds, while Clemmie held her breath, he slowly took a seat at the table.

He stared down at the plate as if he could see it. Often she had to remind herself he couldn't. He seemed so familiar with everything, rarely fumbling in his actions, which came steady and sure.

"Roast. . .potatoes. . .carrots. . .onions. . ." He quietly ticked off the food groups. The aroma of the meal permeated the cabin, which is how he must have known each one.

"Yes and a special surprise for dessert."

"Oh?" His tone wasn't exactly inviting, but neither did it condemn.

"Strawberry shortcake! With real cream."

She had hoped her declaration would at least bring a smile. Instead he became very still and frowned.

"Why would you think that was my favorite?"

"It's not?"

"I never told Thea. As a matter of fact, I never told her any of it. Or Herbert."

Clemmie sucked in a breath. They'd taken care of him for over a year and didn't know his favorite foods? "I—but—h–he mentioned he grew up with you. A–at the refuge. He probably remembered from that." She swallowed, her conscience uneasy at her little deceit. But Joel couldn't find out her identity yet. Things were still so rocky between them. She forced her tone to achieve calm and not stutter. "If those aren't your favorites, I apologize. It's still delicious food."

He grunted something in reply and, to her relief, picked up the fork. His other hand searched the other side of his plate, brushed over a spoon, then came to rest on the table in a loose fist. Intently she watched him spear a piece of roast, scowl, and take a bite.

"I'm not an invalid or a baby," he said.

"Excuse me?"

"You don't have to cut up my food for me. I'm perfectly capable of using a knife. You don't have to keep them out of my reach."

"Oh." Her face warmed. "I wasn't trying to do any such thing. I—I was only trying to help."

He expelled a low breath and gave a reluctant nod.

After his first few bites, the revolutions of his fork from plate to mouth steadily increased until he was practically shoveling food inside. Happy just to stand and watch him now that the lion was calm for once, her eyes feasting on his person after having been deprived so long, she waited until he finished with dessert. Silently she congratulated herself that for a man who claimed he wasn't hungry, he'd just managed to consume his meal in under five minutes.

She gathered the empty dishes. "I might be a little late tomorrow. I'm shopping with a friend."

He didn't respond but, for once, didn't tell her not to bother returning.

Clemmie smiled. It wasn't much, but it was a start.

six

Clemmie turned the page, her mind absorbed in the fictional and fantastical world of angels and monsters.

"Must you be so loud with that?"

Startled into the present, she looked across the table where Joel sat, brooding.

"Must you be so dour all the time?" she shot back. "If you knew how to use that tongue in your head to converse instead of just snap at people, maybe we could have a decent conversation for once, and I wouldn't have to resort to keeping my mind occupied with reading."

He growled in disgust and crossed his arms over his chest, turning his head away.

Earlier in the week she'd brought another chair from Thea's house so she could sit, too. At the moment, however, she was sorely tempted to vacate the chair and his dismal company and escape to pleasant surroundings. Only the rain prevented her departure. What had begun fifteen minutes ago in a sudden downpour effectively trapped her inside his cage. Usually she left the door open when she visited his shed, for fresh air and better lighting than what the lamp could give; today she'd needed to close the door to block out the torrential downpour.

She also felt like growling.

During the past week, relations between them had been stormy but did have calmer moments. Moments when he didn't yell at her or throw things but accepted her presence as a master begins to accept a new servant hired without his approval or knowledge. After days of working for Joel and talking with Thea, Clemmie had learned such erratic mood swings and fits of temper were normal patterns for Joel. The doctor who'd attended him warned to expect such behavior because of whatever caused the pressure to his brain. He never physically harmed her, though. Even when he threw things her way, he always missed, and she wondered if his misses were intentional, meant only to frighten her away, since he always seemed shockingly on target with every other action. His acerbic words, however, found their mark and stung only because Joel said them.

Yet she had formed an invisible armor long ago at the refuge, with the many young hoodlums the judge ordered there, most of them coming from living off the street and impolite society, so she managed to let his insults bounce off her, too—when she wasn't snapping back at him. A fault of hers, responding in kind. Because of their shared history, of which he was still unaware, Joel had the ability to hit the nerve that controlled her cross nature every time.

She had passed the one-week trial period, and much to her surprise, he hadn't terminated her employment as he'd threatened. She didn't ask why, not wanting to tamper with a good thing and possibly cause the tide to turn against her favor. Right now, however, she would give her classic book collection in exchange for the sun to return so she could retreat from his maddening company.

The day had not started well. One thing after another went wrong, and she'd been late to arrive, to find Thea also out of sorts, not wanting to talk, and the children both crying. Clemmie's mood had already been topping the red zone of her emotional thermometer. Add to that, Joel had been the epitome of churlish disdain from the moment she walked inside.

Out of sheer spite, she turned the page, making sure to rustle it loudly. She turned another. And another. . .

"Just what kind of book are you reading?" Joel groused after the sixth turn. "A child's primer?"

Confused by such a question, she stopped mid-page rustle. "What do you mean?"

"There must be only one paragraph on a page for you to

turn them so constantly."

She wasn't sure why, but she laughed. Her mood lightened a bit—surprisingly thanks to Joel's dry words—and she felt a twinge of guilt for acting so childishly. "I'm reading a book my mother gave me. *The Pilgrim's Progress.*"

"That sounds familiar."

She told him a little of what it was about, and he cut her off mid-sentence, sounding almost civil. "I remember that one."

"You read it?"

"Don't sound so surprised. I do—or at least did—read." His tone came out wry again.

She thought of asking why he'd never tried Braille or even suggesting he start but decided against it, not wanting him to slip back into a brooding silence. "Was it for a school assignment?" She asked the first thing that came to mind.

"No. I did read but not that one. I heard someone else read it. The lady who ran the refuge. She had a friend, a viscountess who visited from England one year, shortly after I came home on furlough. Strange thing that. . ." His voice trailed off. "They weren't always chums, more like enemies. At least I know they weren't friendly with one another when they sailed on the *Titanic.*"

Clemmie held her breath during his explanation, realizing he was talking about her mother. "Oh?"

"Interesting story. Mrs. Lyons—only she wasn't married then—robbed the viscountess of a family heirloom. In the end she got it back and forgave Mrs. Lyons. Later she donated the necklace to help in funding the refuge. They became good friends after that. She gave Mrs. Lyons a copy of that book when she visited the States. Mrs. Lyons had developed a habit of reading classics to the children once a week, and I joined in a few nights to listen. Not that I remember much. I heard maybe three chapters before my leave was up." He shrugged.

Clemmie caressed the cover of the old book, realizing this must be the same copy Lady Annabelle had given her mother. She'd been twelve at the time and had greatly admired the soft-spoken, regal woman who braved her fear of sinking ships to cross an ocean again with her husband, Lord Caldwell.

"Would you like me to read to you?" The words were out of her mouth before she could hold them back. Worried he might take her offer wrong, she fumbled to add, "to help pass the time. Since you never heard the rest of the story."

When he didn't speak, she closed the book. "It was only a suggestion. Forget I mentioned it. I just thought it might—"

"Okay."

"What?"

His brow went up. "Have you forgotten your question so soon?"

"Of course not. Do you mean you *would* like me to read to you? Or to forget it?"

"Is that the question you asked?"

She hissed a breath through her teeth. "Must you always make things so difficult, Joel Litton? Can't you just give me a straight answer?"

His mouth twitched in what she thought might become a smile. "All right. Read to me, Marielle."

She blinked. "Is that an order?"

"Did it sound like one?"

"Doesn't it always?"

Joel laughed, and Clemmie forgot to breathe.

It was the first time she'd heard him laugh since their days together at the refuge, and the deep, rich sound of his spontaneous laughter warmed her spirit, soothing away all the previous hurt and angst he'd caused.

"*Please* read to me." His tone slightly mocked, but his voice came soft and silken, his entreaty matching his expression.

Clemmie hoped she could make her vocal cords work, and if they did, she prayed her voice would sound normal. She felt suddenly flushed and out of kilter. How could the room at once feel so hot when the clouds were pouring chilled water outside?

She opened the book to the first chapter.

Joel tucked his hands beneath his armpits, tilting his head back to rest his neck on the tall chair rim as her quiet, husky voice washed over him. She had a beautiful voice. . . warm, gentle when she wasn't upset with him, and Joel was reminded of the place where he grew up and the people there.

In the week and a half she had worked for him, the manner in which he heard her say a few words or trite phrases of Darcy's or Brent's or Charleigh's, the same words that he and Herbert also unintentionally adopted, reminded him of his past at the farm. That must be how she knew such sayings, being around Thea and Herbert. Or maybe they were more popular than he realized.

While she spoke of the quest of a man named Pilgrim and the descriptions of the strange beings he encountered, he found himself wondering what she looked like. If one could match voice to appearance, she was tall for a woman with a self-assured poise. Dark hair. Darker eyes. Deep brown and mysterious, ones that could see right through to a person's soul and not let him get away with anything. He was surprised he could remember color; so much else had faded from his memory.

"Are you even listening?"

Startled out of his thoughts, he gave an involuntary jump.

"What?"

"You're not listening," she gently accused. "Were you sleeping? Your eyes were closed."

He heard her little gasp of remorseful awareness and grinned bitterly. "Not that it matters either way, but no, I wasn't sleeping."

"I'm sorry."

He brushed aside her weak apology, not wanting to dwell on the reason for it. "That's enough reading for one day."

"But I haven't finished the second chapter!"

"It's stopped raining. I'm sure you want to get out of here while you can."

"Would you rather I did?"

"Isn't that what you want?"

"I'd like to stay."

Her quiet admission confused him. "Why? I'm not what you could call good company."

"I like being with you. When you're nice."

He snorted a laugh. "If you were to tally up the occurrences of me being 'nice' over the past week and a half, the scales wouldn't exactly tip in my favor."

She exhaled in exasperation. "That's your choice. You can be nice when you choose to be. And when you are, you're pleasant to be around."

He scoffed. "Why care so much?"

"Pardon?" A sudden hitch tightened her voice.

"Why do you care what the blind man feels? Why do you even want to be around me?"

For a moment he didn't think she would answer. When she did, her words snapped with exasperation, and he sensed she held back the extent of her anger. "That's your problem in a nutshell, Joel Litton. You have this crazy idea that your condition makes you some sort of leper of the human race. And that's so far from the truth, as east is from the west. The only handicap putting up barriers to people wanting to be around you is your constant boorish attitude and spiteful behavior."

"Is that so?"

"Yes, that's so."

He could picture her crossing her arms in belligerence, not willing to back down. Rather than spar further he decided he'd had enough.

"You can go now."

"You're kicking me out?"

"If you want to call it that, fine." Her silence prodded him to add, "It's getting late. You shouldn't walk home in the dark."

He heard her sudden intake of breath. "It's nice of you to care."

Her words came out uncertain, almost a whisper, and for some reason they rubbed him the wrong way. "If you got mugged or worse, it'd be hard on Thea. She'd blame herself."

"Well, at least you care about *someone's* feelings."

He couldn't help but smile at her dry remark. He listened to the rustles and clinks of her gathering her things and the dishes from his meal. Her footsteps tapped to the door. "All right. I'll go. We wouldn't want Thea to feel any unnecessary guilt should anything happen to me." The door creaked open.

"Marielle?"

A few seconds elapsed before she answered. "Yes?"

"Bring that book when you come tomorrow."

seven

Seven little words, but they had the power to boost Clemmie's outlook on Operation Save Joel. For the first time in almost two weeks, she glimpsed an elusive ray of hope. Not only had he not ordered her out, he'd almost given his consent for her return by stating she would come and had expressed a desire for her to read to him again. It wasn't much, but it was progress.

Yet while the situation had mellowed between her and Joel and they had achieved workable boundaries, if not a friendship, one irritating factor dampened this new turn of events. Thea broached it before Clemmie had a chance to leave the following evening.

"You still haven't told him who you are, have you?" Thea shook her head, answering her own question. "Of course you haven't. If you had, things wouldn't be so quiet around here. Joel would have gotten in a lather by now."

"Is that what you want?" Clemmie regarded her, unflinching. "For Joel to get upset? Because that's what'll happen. And then I'd never be able to talk him into it."

"Into what? The operation?"

"Yes. No. . .maybe." Clemmie spread her hands, in an attempt to explain. "It's about so much more than an operation. It's about getting on with living again. Joel has given up, and I want to know why. I think this goes deeper than just bitterness over his physical condition."

"And you don't think asking him as Clemmie would be the same?"

"Asking him as Clemmie will get me the bum's rush, booted out the door."

Thea took a seat at the table. "Then let me ask you this:

What makes the future any different? What makes you think it wouldn't be even worse?"

"Pardon?"

"He'll know at some point. You can't go on lying to him forever. And then he'll feel betrayed."

Clemmie flinched at the word *lying*, and her heart dropped at *betrayed*. She knew speaking falsely was wrong, but in extenuating circumstances, some deceit could be helpful, couldn't it? Her own mother had assumed another identity after being rescued from the *Titanic*, in order to evade the man who'd almost killed her. If she'd given her real name for the survivors' list instead of the name of one of many who had drowned that night, would she be alive today?

"It's complicated."

Thea threw her hands up in exasperation. "It's going to be a whole lot more complicated if you continue with this ruse. Joel may be a lot of things right now, but he's not dumb. Have you thought of this: What if he finds out before you can tell him?"

A piercing scream came from nearby, followed by a wail of pain. Clemmie jumped in her chair, and Thea was up and down the hallway in a flash.

Soon Thea reappeared with her youngest, leading her by the hand. A knotted kerchief hung loosely around Loretta's neck as if it had been a blindfold. Fresh blood trickled from a minor cut on her knee. Thea set her trembling daughter on a kitchen chair and went to wet a towel.

"What happened, sweetheart?" She knelt in front of her and pressed the compress to her knee. "You've been having so many accidents lately."

The child sniffled, wincing as Thea cleaned the cut. "I—I wanted to see what it'd be like."

"What what would be like?"

"To be Uncle Joel."

Clemmie drew in a sharp breath and exchanged a look with Thea.

"I thought I could do better and not fall down. But I can't remember where everything is. I fell on my blocks. They hurted and poked my knee."

The doorbell rang.

"You've got your hands full." Feeling suddenly flustered, Clemmie offered, "I'll get that."

Hannah stood outside the front door like a godsend. "Mother and I finished with things at the bazaar early this evening and thought you might need a lift." Clemmie noticed the chauffeur sitting outside in the Rolls.

"Yes, let me grab my things."

Inside the kitchen she said a quick farewell to Thea.

"Remember what we talked about," Thea said somberly, glancing up at Clemmie.

"How could I forget? Bye, Loretta." She forced a smile. "I hope you feel better soon."

Farewells made, Clemmie hurried to the car. All during the drive, while listening to Hannah's bubbly conversation, her mind revolved around what Loretta had said as she tried to block out Thea's more sobering words. Three conversations, two of them silent, made it difficult to concentrate, and she asked Hannah to repeat herself more than once.

At dinner that night, Clemmie tried to participate in the conversation with Hannah's family and share in their excitement about the upcoming fair, but she could barely follow the discussion. Her mind was still back in Thea's kitchen.

"Is everything all right, dear?" Hannah's mother asked. "You seem not quite yourself this evening."

Clemmie managed a reassuring smile. "I'm just tired."

"I understand you've been hard at work helping Thea during this summer break. A sweet thing to do, but not very restful. Why not turn in early, and I can send you up some hot tea?"

"Thank you. That sounds lovely." Clemmie's gaze dropped to the table. She felt a little remorseful for swearing Hannah to secrecy regarding Joel. Hannah's mother still had no idea he lived a few miles away.

Once Clemmie had returned to her bedroom, she closed the door, leaving the light off. Moonlight seeped through the thin curtains while she remained in shadow. Remembering little Loretta, she grabbed her scarf from a dresser drawer, tying it around her eyes.

Darkness swallowed her, entombing her within a strange, empty well of silence that affected all her senses. She put her hands out, carefully edged forward on the rug then stopped.

Trying to remember the room's layout, she turned toward the window, where the scantest amount of moonlight could be seen through the scarf folds. Thea had told her Joel could differentiate between degrees of shadow, so he did see some variation of light, just not a lot. Slowly Clemmie edged that way.

The toe of her pump snagged on something—the fringe end of the rug?—and she lost her balance. Her palms slapped against hardwood, saving her face from taking the brunt of the fall. Her heart beating fast and erratic, she resisted the impulse to tear away the scarf so she could see. Instead she gathered her wits, letting her breathing calm down.

An anxious sort of vulnerability descended on her as she got to her stinging hands and throbbing knees, struggling to stand. Once upright she slipped out of her pumps and inched forward again, her hands reaching out in front of her. Her fingers met with the bedpost, and she curled them around the carved wood like an anchor, relieved to find something familiar, to gain an idea of where she stood.

The wood beneath her stockings was cool and smooth, and she resisted the impulse to slide her feet along the floor. Any confidence that returned swiftly disintegrated when something sharp pricked the sole of her foot.

"Ow!" she cried out, bending down and raising her foot to grab it. The motion unsteadied her again, and she landed with a thump on her rear.

The sound of the door swinging open preceded the flash of illumination beyond the scarf as the wall sconce flashed on.

"Clemmie?" Hannah asked in surprise. "Are you okay? I heard you yell out. . . ." A dull *click* followed as Hannah set what Clemmie guessed was her tea on the bedside table. Her footsteps drew close. "What on earth are you doing? Playing blindman's bluff solo?"

Clemmie pulled the scarf away, her expression grave as she looked up at her friend. "We have to help him, Hannah."

"Him?" Hannah knelt down. "You mean Joel?" Her gaze lowered. "What happened to your foot?"

Clemmie inspected her sole, pulling out a tiny splinter. She ran her palm along that area of the floor, finding it rough. Of all the places on the smooth planks, she'd found the one area that was eroding. Hannah noticed it, too.

"I'll tell Uncle about that. This place is old. Sorry you got hurt."

"I'm all right. It's Joel I'm worried about." Clemmie had battled with fear, uncertainty, and vulnerability for mere minutes; Joel dealt with this every second of his life. Knowing that, she could begin to understand him a little better. At the refuge, he'd been the leader and all the boys had idealized him, looking up to him. To have all control ripped from him must have been devastating.

Hannah's eyes were sympathetic. "When you first told me about finding him and wanting to help, I told you I was in favor of the idea and would do what I could. I meant that. I don't know, maybe God really is behind this and I'm not the only one who wanted you to visit Connecticut. I think He wanted you here, too. For Joel's sake."

"Then you don't think I'm wrong to conceal my identity in order to help him?"

"I didn't say that. But Clemmie—and don't get sore." Hannah hesitated. "If you have to keep asking and always trying to get affirmation from others, maybe it's you who doesn't believe it's the right thing to do. And maybe you don't need to be told the answer by anyone else after all."

Clemmie didn't want to hear or acknowledge such sound advice. She wished she could phone her mother and seek her counsel, but she didn't want to breach any slim and grudging trust Joel had given by telling others his location; that was his responsibility. Or maybe—God help her, and she prayed for His guidance each night—maybe the true reason she chose not to ring home was the worry over what her mother might say about Clemmie's ruse. She hoped she wasn't making a royal mess of things.

&

Joel settled back in his chair and closed his eyes. It didn't matter if he did or didn't close them, as far as blocking out the world went, but it did help him relax. Marielle's voice also relaxed him when she wasn't scolding him. To be fair, she only snapped back when he initiated the arguments, which this past week had been sporadic, to his surprise and hers.

He hadn't thought he could feel comfortable around anyone again, but something about Marielle reminded him of the only home he'd known. Maybe that's why he hadn't refused her staying the extra hours after her family expressed concern over her walking home near dark every evening and told her to wait for someone to come and collect her. She hadn't wanted to get in the way of supper and other family doings once Herbert arrived home from work, so she'd stayed at Joel's shed of a home, even sharing his meals. He had demanded solitude for mealtimes in the past, so to have a dinner guest was disconcerting at first, but he'd grown accustomed to her company. To pass the time, she read to herself or to him from her book, as she did now.

Joel's mind, however, had strayed far from the wanderings of Pilgrim. Not for the first time he wondered about his storyteller.

"You're not listening." She heaved a sigh. "Have you had enough for today?"

"Tell me," he mused aloud, "what do you look like?"

She gasped, and he could imagine her shock. He'd never posed any personal question to her, though she'd shown no hesitation to grill him.

"Does it matter?" She hedged in giving a straight answer, which puzzled him.

"Maybe not, but fair is fair. You can see me. Why shouldn't I at least be allowed to draw a picture of you in my mind?"

"I guess I see your point."

He grinned at her reluctance. "I never would have thought you were shy."

"I'm not. I just don't like talking about myself."

"Humor me this once."

"Oh very well." The leather binding creaked as she closed the book. Her skirt rustled as she fidgeted in her chair. "What do you want to know?"

"Let's start with hair and eye color," he suggested drolly.

"My hair is a sort of light brownish, sort of reddish. My eyes are a greenish sort of grayish."

"Sounds colorful," he drawled at her unenthusiastic admission. "Any freckles?"

"What?" Her question came sharp. "Why do you ask?"

"The few redheads I've known have them." He wondered if she was as sensitive about her freckles as those girls were.

"Can we talk about something else, please?"

"You really don't like talking about yourself, do you?" He might not be able to see her, but he could sense her apprehension.

"I'm not that interesting."

"I disagree." He deliberated. "I'd place you at about five foot five. Am I close?"

She gasped again, and he assumed his guess was correct.

"How could you possibly know? I mean, w–we've never. . . touched. Or—or anything." Her voice came soft, nervous.

"When you stand in front of me, I not only hear your voice, I feel the level of it. It comes to just below my collarbone."

"Oh."

At her quiet reply he added, "I told you before, my other senses have kicked in and sharpened since the accident that got me this way. I sense a lot of things about you."

"Speaking of sharpened, you could really use a haircut," she squeaked out quickly. "And a shave."

"Changing the subject?"

"Stating a fact. Unless your plan was to imitate a Viking? Or maybe a bum? That's quite a beard you've grown. It's the only thing saving you from others mistaking you for a girl, with how long your hair has gotten."

Instead of riling him, it made him laugh. "Why should I care how I look? I'm not going anywhere."

"Maybe you should. It's not healthy to stay cooped up in this shed or to limit your excursions to your sliver of a porch."

He folded his arms across his chest. "Nice try. But this conversation isn't about me. I just realized that in the four weeks since you've invaded my privacy, I've learned very little about you."

She cleared her throat. "Well, I like the great outdoors. Speaking of, did you know the county fair is starting up next weekend? The weekend before the bazaar my friend is working at."

"If that was a ploy to get my mind off track, it didn't work. Where are you from, Marielle? Where do you go after you leave here?"

"Is it so important?"

Five minutes ago he might not have cared. But with her evasive responses, Joel realized just how badly he wanted to know. "Yes."

He waited, as rigid and determined as she was silent. She let out a surrendering breath.

"Okay, fine. I'll make a deal with you. Let me trim your hair and give you a shave, and I'll tell you anything you want to know."

"You have got to be joking."

"No, I'm quite serious."

Surprised she would be so adamant about his grooming, he narrowed his eyes in sudden distrust. "And you've done such a thing before? Used a straight razor?"

"Worried?" Her words held an undercurrent of amusement. "Don't be. You're perfectly safe. You wouldn't be the first man I've shaved. And I've cut hair before, too."

"Are you married? Widowed? Divorced?"

"No answers to any more personal questions unless and until you agree to my terms."

He let out a rasping breath of a laugh. "Fine." He didn't care one way or the other how he looked. Neither Thea nor Herbert ever offered to groom him, and he never asked. He bathed regularly so he wouldn't "stink to high heaven," as Darcy used to say, and that was about the sum total of his grooming habits.

Why would he so suddenly think of Darcy and Lyons' Refuge?

"Swell!" He heard his guest hurry to the door and open it. "I'll just get the things I need. I'll be back in two shakes."

Before he could change his mind or stop her, he heard her footsteps whisk outside and hit the porch.

Joel wryly wondered what he'd gotten himself into.

eight

Procuring Herbert's razor and other implements wasn't a problem. But evading Thea's string of questions about Clemmie's intentions took up the entire five minutes she waited in the kitchen for Herbert to retrieve his shaving tools. Thea put her hand to Clemmie's arm before she could whisk back outside.

"Tell him."

"I will. Soon. Just not yet."

"I don't like this, Clemmie. I hope you know what you're doing."

She ignored her conscience agreeing with Thea's assessment and hurried back to Joel, to find him in a brooding mood. No longer dryly amused, he seemed quiet, suspicious. He allowed her to tie a tablecloth around his neck and waited while she whipped up shaving foam. But before she could bring the coated bristles to his face, he grabbed her wrist. She gasped in surprise.

"First things first. How do I know that you know what you're doing?"

"I—I was taught. My uncle doesn't have a steady hand, and my aunt sprained her wrist once," she explained, speaking of Brent and Darcy. "She shaved him before, and when I said I would help, she walked me through the motions. Due to his profession, he needs to keep a clean-cut appearance and felt whiskers made him look too scruffy for an important meeting."

"You lived with your aunt and uncle?"

"They live with us."

He nodded, as if taking it all in. "So you've done this once before."

"Actually, five times."

"There are no barbers left in town for your uncle to run to?"

"I suppose. I—I don't know. Or why he chose not to go to one of them. Look, I do know what I'm doing."

"But you've never shaved a full beard before, am I right?"

"Well, no. . ."

"So maybe you should cut it first."

She smiled wide. "That's an excellent idea! Must be why Herbert included the shears."

At her enlightened enthusiasm, he pushed her wrist away. "Maybe this isn't such a good idea. . . ."

"No. You're stuck with me now, Joel Litton." Determined again, she pushed against his chest when he moved forward to rise then picked up the shears. "No sudden moves, or I won't be held responsible." She made cutting noises, pumping the handles to stress her point. He grew as still as a block of wood.

Amused to suddenly have the lion as docile as a kitten, she snipped at the light brown curls covering his jaw, careful not to graze his skin. She didn't even sense him breathing and was surprised she herself didn't tremble. This was the closest she'd been to Joel since their days at the refuge. But she'd learned from her mother to keep focused on a task, despite any distractions, and see it through to the end. She imagined that's what helped her concentrate on playing barber and not think too much about being so close to him, actually touching him. . . .

Focus, Clemmie, focus!

Once the beard was manageable, she lathered up his jaw.

"When do you fulfill your end of the bargain?" He softly spit out lather that had gotten in his mouth when he opened it to speak.

"Do you really want me to concentrate on answering personal questions when I've got a razor at your throat?"

"Good point. I'll wait. But before you start, I've got one question, and it won't wait."

"Okay," she said uneasily.

"Why is this so important to you? Why do you even care?"

"Maybe I just want to see what you look like beneath that lion's mane you've been hiding behind."

He snorted a laugh. "Not the answer I expected."

"But it'll do?" she asked hopefully.

His eyes were intense, like clear blue crystals. They seemed to see through her, and she reminded herself yet again that he was blind and couldn't pick up on the anxiety in her eyes or how she nervously bit her lip, afraid he would discover all her secrets.

"For now." He settled back, leaning the nape of his neck against the chair rim. "So if you're going to do this thing, let's get it over with."

"Your wish is my command, good sir." Slowly, so slowly, she made her first swipe with the razor.

He was the epitome of cooperation, remaining so still she wondered if he'd fallen asleep. She didn't rush through the task, fearful of leaving even the tiniest nick, and felt thankful he hadn't asked if she'd ever cut Brent.

At last she slid the razor along his jaw one final time, set it down near the bowl of warm water, wiped his face with a dry towel, and observed the entirety of her handiwork. She couldn't help the gasp that escaped her lips—she'd forgotten just how handsome he was. With his hair still touching his shoulders, he looked more like a warrior angel than ever before, every feature of his face appearing as if it were sculpted by the finest artisan.

"What is it?" he asked tersely. "What's the matter?"

"N–nothing."

His winged brows drew together. "You don't sound like it's nothing. What have you done to me?"

"I told you, nothing. You're fine. Not a scratch on you. I—I just realized I forgot a hot towel. I—I was supposed to put that on your face first, I think, though I did wet it." Her heart pounding from nerves, she took a hasty step in retreat, but he reached out and grabbed her arm, hauling her forward as though she might run for the door. The abruptness of his move unbalanced her and caused her to topple to his lap.

Shocked motionless, neither of them spoke or moved for endless seconds. She didn't breathe. And he didn't let her go. His other strong arm moved around her middle, trapping her in a rigid embrace.

"You're not going anywhere until you answer some questions."

His voice rumbled against the palm she'd pressed to his chest when she fell. She snatched it away. "I—I. . ." She worked to keep her voice low and even. "What is it you want to know?"

He tilted his head, his blank eyes on her. "Why are you so nervous if you didn't do anything wrong?"

Her lips parted in disbelief. He really needed to ask? Did he feel nothing of the same surge of emotions from holding her against him? She'd never been this close to a man who wasn't a relative and felt the blood rush to her head, warming her entire body.

"If I had made a mistake and slipped, don't you think you would be feeling the pain by now?"

He seemed to consider. "Okay, I'll give you that." But he didn't let her go. She fidgeted a little to remind him of her predicament. Her action had the opposite effect as his arm tightened around her.

"I told you. You're not going anywhere till I get answers."

Her heart pounded harder, if that were possible. "Answers to what?"

"For starters, where do you live?"

She gave an almost hysterical breath of laughter. Did he not trust her enough to keep her end of the bargain, feeling he had to hold her prisoner to answer such questions?

"A few miles from here."

"And about what I asked before. Are you married?"

"No."

"Widowed? Divorced?"

"No and no."

She felt the tension drain from him slightly. His hold on her relaxed, but still he didn't release her.

"How old are you, anyway?"

"It's not polite to ask a lady her age."

He snorted. "Since when did I come across as being polite? Well?" he insisted when she didn't speak. "It's hardly fair since I can't see you to make my own guess."

"Nearing eighteen."

"You're just a baby!"

"No, I'm a woman," she said stiffly.

"And I'm an old bachelor nearing thirty. What do you think of that?"

What did she think of that? She'd only kept a record of his birthday every year since she'd been old enough to mark the date on the calendar. "Thirty's not old."

He grunted as if not pleased with her response. "So, you live with your family?"

"Yes."

"And what do they think of their daughter walking across town every day to tend to a blind recluse?"

"Everyone I've told supports me."

"Everyone you've told?" His brow lifted.

"Yes." She fidgeted again, trying not to tell a lie, though the deceit of her ruse made it difficult.

"In other words, your parents don't know."

"I didn't say that."

"Do they?"

"Does it matter? I'm old enough to make my own decisions. I don't need their permission. And besides, I'm not doing anything wrong."

"You sure about that? I think maybe you're hiding something."

His words came laced with suspicion and prickled at her conscience.

"Seriously? You think I'm hiding some terrible dark secret?

That I have a skeleton in my closet?" She tried to make her voice sound light and confused, humorous even, but it came out strained. "Why? What have I ever done to make you feel that way?"

But as she said the false words, they only made her feel worse. This was all wrong. Hannah was right. Thea was right. One lie begat another, and she was tired of always needing to cover her tracks. She must confess, hope he would forgive her, and pray he wouldn't shut her out of his life. She opened her mouth to try to find the right words to explain, but his fingers tentatively touched her lips before she could.

"No. Don't. You're right. You've been nothing but helpful, even when I was a real jerk, and I'm sorry. You don't have to answer any more questions. And you sure shouldn't have to defend yourself to me. I'm the last person to act as judge and jury."

She wondered what he meant by that remark but couldn't think straight as, feather light, his fingertips trailed her bottom lip in the act of slowly pulling them away. "I just hope I'm not wrong about you."

The mood between them changed, her every sensation intensely felt as she teetered high on an emotional seesaw.

"I"—she breathed against his fingertips—"don't know what you want me to say."

"Say nothing." His lips covered hers, stealing any words and every breath.

She had often wondered what it would be like to receive Joel's kiss, ever since she was a young girl. The reality of her dream shook her to the core of her soul.

The lime scent and taste from the specks of remaining shaving cream mingled with the heat of his mouth on hers, all of it making her lightheaded and strangely warm inside and out. She clung to his shoulders as if she might fall, when suddenly he pushed her away and leaned back, holding her far from him.

"I shouldn't have done that." He momentarily remained

frozen then practically shoved her from his lap. She forced her wobbly legs to stand. "This was wrong." He shook his head, clearly angry. With her, with himself, she didn't know. "Look, I think it would be better if you just left and didn't come ba—"

"I'm not upset," she hurried to say before he could finish and throw her out for good. "And—and I want you to know. I've decided how you can pay me back."

"What?" Confused, he shook his head at her abrupt change of topic. "What do you mean, pay you back?"

"When I first started working for you, you said you didn't feel right about not giving me wages." She was surprised she could speak rationally, as addled as she felt by the memory of his touch and kiss, both of which she could still feel traces, and she had to hold to the table's rim to remain steady. "I know exactly how you can pay me."

❧

"Well?" Joel asked when she didn't elaborate. "I'm waiting."

"Take me to the county fair."

Her preposterous words at first didn't connect. When they did, he snorted in disbelief that she would suggest such a thing. "Are you off your nut? That's impossible!"

"Why?"

"Why? *Why!*" He worked to get his temper in check. "In case you've forgotten, I'm blind."

"You have two good legs, don't you? Use your cane."

"No." He winced at the thought of the blind man's stick that stood unused in the corner.

"Why not? You're the one being impossible."

"How can you say such a thing to me? Do you know what it's like to live like this? It's not your eyes that were struck blind. Do you know what it's like to step off a stair and walk into the unknown? To be literally in the dark? To have people stop and stare at the pathetic wretch, wondering if he'll trip and fall?"

"How do you know they're staring if you can't see them?"

Her voice had gone quiet and subdued. "From what I understand, you were never one to care what strangers think about you. And if you're really all that concerned, I can be your eyes."

"I said no!" He flung his hand sideways in an arc. Without meaning to, he felt it connect with the bowl. It crashed to the floor. "See what mistakes a blind man can make? Now beat it before I get really upset."

Her footsteps were steady as she did the opposite, moving toward him. He heard the bowl scrape wood as she picked up the shattered pieces.

"Leave it."

"I can't just leave this on the floor for you to step on."

"I'll take care of it. You could cut your hand."

"Nice of you to care, but I've had to clean up worse messes than this when my younger brothers had one of their little tantrums."

He pulled his lips in a tight line. "So, you think I'm throwing a tantrum?"

"Yes I do. You're so full of self-pity, it's a wonder you don't drown in it."

He snorted in exasperation. "Will you just get out of here?"

"We're not finished. I haven't cut your hair."

"I've had enough of your help for one night."

She paused. "Fine. We'll resume tomorrow, and I'm not taking no for an answer." Her steps moved to the door, paused, then turned around and came back. "Before I go, there's one thing I don't understand."

"What's that?" he bit out through clenched teeth.

"If you're so unhappy with the way things have been and so dissatisfied with life as it is now, why don't you agree to the operation?"

Incredulous anger made his face burn hot. "Thea had no right to tell you about that!"

"Don't blame Thea. I got curious and asked. I guess you could say I almost forced the information from her."

He slammed his fist on the table. "Well, stay out of my affairs! It's none of your business!"

"I understand there's an element of risk involved," she persisted, "but you were never the type of man to run from danger. Even as a boy, you never retreated from a challenge. Even life-threatening ones, though I understand this doesn't qualify. In fact, you were usually the first one to jump into trouble, feet first."

He narrowed his eyes at her correct assessment of his character, though she had the logistics of the doctor's findings wrong. "How do you know so much about me or what I'm like?"

"Herbert talks about the old days quite often."

He snorted in derision. "Another person who should keep his big trap shut and his opinions to himself."

"And I've built my own evaluation of your character in the month that I've been here." She continued as if she'd not heard him. "One thing you're not is a coward. So why didn't you go through with the operation, if there's a chance you could see again? Why don't you go through with it now? You're clearly not happy."

"Thanks for the psychoanalysis, doc, but for the last time, mind your own potatoes and keep out of my business."

"Is it that you have no one to help you financially? No friends or family?"

"I'm not a charity case!"

"There are such things as loans."

"In these hard times? Look, just leave it—and me—alone."

"You asked me questions. Don't I have the right to do the same?"

She wasn't backing down, and rather than argue further, he felt weary of the whole subject. "Go home, Marielle. I'm tired and want to turn in for the night."

"A shave exhausted you so much?"

He heard the skepticism in her voice.

"Having a veritable stranger hold a razor to your throat

does tend to wear on a man's nerves," he countered dryly.

"That's all I still am to you then? A stranger?"

He couldn't mistake the sadness in her words. But that was all she could ever be to him. He couldn't afford to get involved, no matter how phenomenal it had felt to hold and kiss her. It had been well over a year since he'd been so close to a woman, but she had a rare quality he couldn't pinpoint that separated her from the rest.

Even so, he had nothing to offer, and she had no reason to want to give him an opportunity. He was only a curiosity to her. A charity case upon whom she wished to dole out her good deeds and brandish compassion. Even if she was interested in more, once the novelty wore off, she certainly wouldn't want to find herself trapped in a relationship with a man who couldn't see and would always need some sort of guidance.

She'd been accurate in most of her assumptions regarding his character, but she was wrong about one thing. He didn't pity himself for his condition. He deserved no man's pity. But he did warrant all the blame.

"Go home, Marielle," he said tiredly.

"Then you agree?"

"No, but you can't spend the night here, and I'm going to bed."

"Fine." He heard her huff of exasperation. "But this isn't over, Joel Litton."

He ignored her declaration. "As long as you insist on using both my names all the time, you might as well save yourself the trouble and just use the one."

"Litton?"

He couldn't help the faint smile that quirked his mouth at her teasing. "Joel."

"All right." Pleasure softened her voice. "Good night, Joel."

He laid his head back without answering and closed his eyes. At the soft click of the door, he knew he was again alone.

"Good night, pixie angel. I don't know whether to call you a menace or a saint. Just who are you, Marielle?"

It was then he realized he didn't even know her last name.

nine

It took four visits to convince Joel to change his mind. For every reason he gave that he couldn't go to the fair, Clemmie offered a solution showing that the outing was not impossible for him—as he claimed—but probable, even preferable. He needed to get out of the house and into the world.

Thea offered her support, and Herbert announced they would make it a family outing. Hannah talked to her mother, both of them overburdened with work for the upcoming bazaar, and Hannah's mother gladly relinquished the chauffeur for a day, eager to help when Clemmie broke down and told her of Joel's presence in town. Sworn to secrecy, Hannah's mother also expressed concern that Clemmie was keeping her identity from Joel, but Clemmie assured her hostess she would tell him soon. And at last, with no further arguments, Joel curtly agreed to attend the fair, though his mood grew dour the rest of that afternoon.

She hadn't realized it would be so difficult. Not just to conceal her identity but to continue in her plan to help him. Some days everything proceeded smoothly, and she felt the heavens smiled upon her—that God, indeed, had orchestrated her arrival to Connecticut, and she was following through with His plans. She'd even begun to hope for her girlhood dream to come true, realizing she'd never gotten over wanting to be more than Joel's friend, no matter how hard she tried to convince herself and everyone else she was long over her infatuation. Only this didn't feel like the old silly schoolgirl fascination.

His unexpected kiss had brought her buried feelings back into glaring relief; she had to stop lying to herself and especially to him. Still, every time she considered how to tell him she was Clemmie, her mind played out the scenario of what would ensue. No matter how many ways she imagined it, the ending always remained the same—they both wound up hurt and losers. She had mired herself in this web of deceit too deeply and didn't know how to gracefully extract herself without breaking the fragile cords of trust that slowly had begun bonding them—and causing her pain.

Those were the days she wondered if she could or should continue the charade, feeling sadly inadequate to help Joel who bore a secret burden he wouldn't share, no matter how she tried to get him to open up to her. But she wasn't a coward, and that's what she would be if she never returned, giving no confession or explanation except for whatever Thea might offer Joel should Clemmie suddenly quit working for him.

And if she did conclude all association with him, wouldn't he feel rejected and betrayed despite his demands that she go, which had been coming less frequently?

When asked, she continued to read her novel to him. One afternoon after they'd both eaten, he was in one of his sullen moods and ordered her to resume their reading. She did— from the book she had open. She'd brought along a Bible, intrigued to find symbolism that was in the allegory of the novel and the verses relating to it. When she started reading where she'd left off, he'd shown surprise not to hear her speak of Pilgrim's progress to the Celestial City. He hadn't ordered her to stop, but his expression had grown hard and shuttered, making his feelings clear with regard to her choice of reading material.

Each evening she shared her frustrations of the day and concerns for Joel's spiritual health with Hannah. And when she retired, she offered supplications to the Lord, asking Him to intervene and bring the lost lamb that Joel had become, however black, back to God's fold. She hurt for him but refused to show pity, knowing it would only make things worse. Instead her pillow bore the brunt of her heartache as, alone in her room, she shed any tears she'd held at bay while in his company.

But this day held no place for tears. The morning shone sunny and bright, full of promise. And Joel, much to her surprise, seemed in a pleasant mood, though he showed some stubbornness in his refusal to use his cane, even just for the walk to the waiting car. She clung to his arm, both to aid him and for the closeness such an action afforded.

Inside the Rolls, despite its roomy nature, the seats were crowded. Any closer and she would have been sitting on his lap. The memory of that moment and what followed made her face go hot, something that Herbert, who sat directly across from her, didn't fail to miss.

"What did you say to Marielle?" he teased Joel from the seat opposite, where Thea and Loretta also sat. "You should see her face—as red as a peony. Almost matches her hair."

"Thanks a bundle for that trite and unnecessary information." Clemmie modulated her voice gently while staring daggers at her old childhood torturer. "But I'll have you know my hair is not that red. It's almost auburn."

"Dream on, little girl."

Thea sharply elbowed him in the ribs, though she couldn't know the extent of damage her husband may have done. Clemmie's heart skipped a beat at the words he often used to say to her when they'd lived at the refuge. She hoped Joel hadn't caught on and gave him a swift glance.

His perfect features, no longer half hidden by facial hair, were a mask, his blue eyes indifferent. She couldn't read his emotions no matter how hard she tried. Herbert realized his error by the deer-struck look on his face and mouthed, "Sorry."

"Well, old man, at least your hair no longer resembles a caveman who hadn't yet invented a comb," he said too robustly. Clemmie rolled her eyes heavenward at his lame tactic to save the moment, and Thea elbowed him again. "What? What did I say? She did a good job is all I meant."

"Enough talk about hair," Thea inserted. "Tell me about this bazaar your friend's mother is holding. I ran across some things yesterday if it's not too late to make a donation."

"I would think the ladies on the committee would be thrilled." Clemmie mouthed a thank-you. "I'll ask about it tonight."

"Mommy," Loretta interrupted, "will there be animals at the fair?"

"I think so, sweetheart. If I remember, fairs have them."

"Have you been to the fair?"

Thea laughed. "It's been many years."

"What about you, Uncle Joel?" Bethany asked.

All eyes turned his way, and Clemmie uneasily thought again how silent he'd become since the drive began. Of all things, this morning he had shocked her speechless when he'd asked her last name! She had literally been saved by the cat when it chose that moment to run between them, and Loretta had given chase.

"When I was a boy, I went to a carnival." His reply came quietly.

"Is a carnival like a fair?"

His grin to Bethany was halfhearted. "Something like it, I guess. I've never been to a county fair."

"What did you do at the carnival?"

"Look, Bethany, see those tents ahead," Herbert pointed out. "We're almost there."

"Yippee!" Loretta bounced on the seat, clapping her hands and earning her mother's admonition to sit still like her big sister.

Clemmie knew about that carnival and understood Herbert's eagerness to change the subject. As an adventurous boy of twelve, Joel had run away from his chaperones and into the path of a dangerous criminal, getting into some of the worst trouble he'd ever been in and also deceiving her parents. Thinking of her own deceit she squirmed almost as much as Loretta.

Joel's hand suddenly clamped down on her knee, startling her into sucking in a huge lungful of air—one she found difficult to release.

❧

The feel of her leg tensing beneath his hand made Joel realize what he'd done. He had initiated his reflexive action to keep her still, but at her shock he quickly withdrew his hand.

"Stop fidgeting," he explained, "or you're going to bruise me black-and-blue." The admonition was extreme. Though they sat with their sides touching, she could hardly bruise him from wriggling around. But he felt every movement she made, even sensed those he didn't physically experience, and to have her so close was doing strange things to his mental faculties, bringing back thoughts of her sitting on his lap and their kiss.

And she had kissed him back that night, though it took days for him to acknowledge it. Did she kiss him out of pity? Curiosity? If for neither of those reasons, what was her motive?

What was his?

His motivation to understand her, to know her, clashed with his reluctance to have anything to do with her, all of his feelings becoming increasingly blurred as the weeks elapsed. Lately she reminded him of someone, though he couldn't place her, and he wondered if he'd met her at a party or an acquaintance's house.

Such a likelihood seemed improbable, because he didn't remember meeting anyone in the month before he went blind who fit Marielle's description. Besides, if they had met before, wouldn't she have mentioned it?

He thought about asking her but was cut off by Loretta's excited squeal, just as he'd been interrupted by the cat's yowl earlier when he'd tried to get Marielle's full name.

"We're here! We're here!"

At the cry that their destination had been reached, Joel's

fears resurfaced. Herbert opened the door on his side while the chauffeur helped the women out the other side. Herbert's hand touched his sleeve, but Joel hung back.

"Come on, old man. Don't dillydally. Need help getting out?"

Joel recognized the teasing the two of them had shared since boyhood, but right now he felt far from joking. "I'm only one year older than you—and don't patronize me!" He whipped his arm away from Herbert's touch. "I should never have agreed to this! It was a mistake."

"Mama." He heard Loretta whisper. "What's wrong with Uncle Joel?"

Suddenly the scent of lilacs strongly assaulted his senses as the woman who'd been both tormentor and savior approached his side. Her fingertips were gentle upon his shoulder.

"You promised to be my escort," she reminded. "Please don't back out now."

Marielle's soft voice calmed him where nothing else could. He offered a curt nod—shocked to feel her arm slip through his once he was standing—but didn't protest.

At first the cane seemed awkward in his hand; he felt vulnerable walking over uneven ground he didn't know and couldn't see. But despite his peevish edginess, she didn't abandon his side or chastise him for his disagreeable behavior.

"Tell me," he said, hearing people hush or talk in undertones as they walked past. "Are they all staring?"

"I assume you mean the ladies?"

Marielle's answer and the tightness in her voice took him aback. "What?"

"You heard me. The ladies." She made as if to move her arm away, but he tightened his grasp, not willing to let her escape without explanation.

"What do you mean by that?"

"I. . ." Her breath hitched as if she were now uneasy. "I understand you were quite a ladies' man."

"And that was your first thought when I asked if anyone was staring?"

"Yes." Her admission came reluctantly.

With a disbelieving laugh he scoffed at her. "Trust me. I'm no longer the object of any woman's admiration. I'm surprised you'd even think it."

"Are you really so stupid?"

The anger in her voice hid the barest trace of tears, and the way her fingers tensed around his sleeve perplexed him.

"Are you all right?"

"Swell." Her voice came steadier. "But since you ask, why do you care if anyone stares? Let's just try and enjoy the day."

He exhaled a frustrated breath. She was right, he supposed. He couldn't see anyone's reactions, and he'd never cared about what people thought before. So why had it become so all-fired important now?

"All right. On one condition."

"You're making a condition to enjoying the day?"

He couldn't help but grin at her amusement.

"You don't baby me or treat me like an invalid, and I won't reconsider hunting down that chauffeur of your friend's to get me out of here."

"All right. It's a deal." She slipped her arm from his, but he grabbed her hand and looped it back where it had been. He sensed her surprise in the sudden trembling of her hand, which he kept under his.

"That I'll allow."

"Oh really?" she asked with a soft laugh.

He smiled.

ten

Joel's bright smile and persistent hold on her arm gave Clemmie a much-needed boost of confidence. She hadn't been jealous, not really, but the curious yet clearly interested looks from young women walking in the opposite direction made her recall the old days, when Joel had only to give one of his engaging boyish grins for the ladies to take notice and nearly swoon where they stood.

For herself, she didn't read more into his action to keep her close than what she assumed it meant. His pride wouldn't allow him to admit he needed help, and clearly he felt nervous without her holding his arm as they strolled over the unfamiliar ground and through the crowds. For him, she would be whatever he needed, though she wished to be so much more.

Relieved the atmosphere had eased between them again, she surveyed her surroundings. Though the fair wasn't much different than the annual one near home, the day seemed brighter, the crowds friendlier, the amusements more interesting, and she felt sure it was because she walked with Joel.

Tents and booths stood scattered in no real order, as if a giant hand had tossed them to land where they may. A fringe of trees provided a backdrop against a sky so blue it almost hurt to look at it. The nearby woods shielded the morning sun, which peeked in scattered rays between thick foliage. Everywhere, she saw smiles and heard laughter, and she silently thanked God again that she'd been able to convince Joel to come, certain such a fun climate would be good medicine for his wounded soul.

She described everything she saw, remembering to be his eyes, and warned him of anything his cane might miss in an offhand manner, so he wouldn't accuse her of coddling him.

Some passersby did openly stare as he searched the ground with his cane for obstacles that might trip him. But she ignored their curiosity, happy that Joel was finally away from his stifling shed and out among the populace again.

"Do I smell hot dogs?"

Clemmie laughed at his sudden boyish enthusiasm and scouted the myriad booths and tents ahead. Far in the distance she spotted a hot dog vendor.

"Can I have a hot dog, Daddy?" Bethany wanted to know.

"We just got here, cupcake!"

"Aw, let the kid have a hot dog if she wants one."

"You're just saying that because you want one," Herbert accused Joel.

"What can I say? Blame my stomach."

"You mean that bottomless pit below your chest?"

"Funny man. I seem to remember you couldn't get enough pies in your day. A habit you never outgrew. Tell me that you don't plan on visiting the pie-eating booth for a contest."

"How'd you know about that, Uncle Joel, if you've never been to a fair?" Bethany interrupted the men's banter. "I don't see any booths with pies."

"I know because your daddy told me there'd be one. Don't worry. If it's there, he'll find it. He has a nose for such things. And a mouth."

The adults chuckled and moved toward the booth. Five minutes later the happy vendor pocketed his change and the group moved away loaded with steaming hot dogs slathered in mustard. A rare treat in such hard times.

"Mmm." Joel angled the end of the bun and meat into his mouth. "This isn't half bad. Almost reminds me of the old picnics at the refuge."

Herbert laughed. "Nowhere near as good as Darcy's cooking though."

"Or her baking. She made some of the best pies while we were growing up."

"Yes, her pies are contest winners," Clemmie mused aloud.

Uneasy silence descended. Joel's arm tensed beneath her hand.

"Or so you've said," she hastily amended. "Right?" She shot a pleading look at Thea and Herbert, who appeared just as apprehensive as they looked between Joel and Clemmie. She also glanced his way. Nothing on his face gave a hint that he'd noticed her slip, and she exhaled in relief.

"My Herbie's always filling us in on tales of your days together at the refuge," Thea answered. "He goes into such vivid detail we feel we've actually lived it. He mentioned that famous fence-painting contest for a pie more than once."

Both men groaned then chuckled, and again the mood eased. But Clemmie noticed the disapproval in Thea's eyes as she glanced her way.

Thea didn't lie, but Clemmie saw her unease at covering over the comment about Darcy's pies. Thea shouldn't have to. Clemmie's well-intentioned ruse had gone on long enough; Joel deserved the truth. They'd grown close enough that perhaps he wouldn't toss her out on her ear once he learned she was "clumsy little Clemmie" as he'd affectionately teased while tweaking her nose or ruffling her hair in her awkward years. She'd grown out of her clumsiness—except when it came to untangling herself from the sticky web of half-truths she'd created.

How could she tell him? Certainly she couldn't do it today. She wasn't about to spoil any memory of his first outing since he'd gone blind. Confessions of the soul must wait. They had to!

"Ewww," Bethany squealed, appalled. "What are they doing?" She pointed to a booth in the distance. A young blond leaned over the booth's rim to plant a kiss on the cheek of a boy at least five years younger. He walked away grinning, his fingers rubbing the red lipstick imprint she'd left on his skin.

Clemmie grinned as Thea covered Loretta's eyes with her hand when an older man pecked the woman on the lips.

"That's called a kissing booth," Herbert said. "And those dandies in line are paying the lady to receive her kiss."

"Ixnay," Thea reproved. "The children."

"It's all for a good cause, dear. Most of the proceeds of the fair are going to help the homeless. I help write the news, remember? Perhaps I should contribute."

Thea grabbed his arm as he teasingly moved in the direction of the booth. "Don't you dare take one step farther, Herbert Miller, or you'll find yourself out in the shed with Joel tonight."

"Aw, honey, you know you're the only gal for me. But maybe Joel would like a turn." He looked at his friend. "Whatta ya say, ole pal? I've never known you to refuse such a worthy cause."

Clemmie waited tensely for Joel's answer.

"I think I'll pass."

"You've got to be joshing me—you pass up a smooch from an attractive dame?"

Thea elbowed Herbert in the ribs, doing what Clemmie wished to do.

"Yeah. Those days are history."

Clemmie didn't know whether to cheer with relief that he wouldn't undertake Herbert's challenge to kiss a stranger or sigh with wretchedness that he now thought himself unfit for a woman to love.

Oh, how she wished to show him differently!

"Yuck." Bethany wrinkled her nose at the kissing booth and looked up at her father. "Can we go find the animals?"

"Sure, cupcake. Whatever you want."

The morning passed into afternoon, both little girls bubbling over with excitement at the fun they shared, especially petting a black baby goat a farmer had brought for children to befriend, along with his prize animals competing for the winning blue ribbons. They laughed when the little kid ate a tin can, and Joel remarked that the animal not only had a bottomless stomach but an ironclad one and that he'd "give Herbert a run for his money on the pies."

Of course then Herbert took up Joel's challenge, much like when they were boys, and entered the contest. They all stood on the sidelines and cheered him on. Bethany giggled.

"What's so funny?" Joel asked.

"They tied Daddy's hands behind him so he'll have to eat the pie just like our cat drinks milk from her bowl!"

Joel grinned. "Now that I'd love to see."

Thus encouraged, amid gales of laughter, Bethany told Joel every detail of the messy endeavor once the contest bell rang.

"I can't see!" Loretta complained from Joel's other side. "I wanna see, too!"

Joel handed Clemmie his cane and reached down, lifting the little girl onto his side so she could witness the messy event above the heads of the adults in front of them.

"Ooo, there's Daddy!" she squealed, pointing and giggling, bouncing up and down on Joel's hip. "His face is all blue with berries!"

Clemmie smiled to watch Joel with the children. They clearly had a fondness for him, and he didn't appear to dislike them as she'd once thought.

Herbert finished his pie in record time. Thea wiped berry juice from his cheeks and chin, chiding the girls who crowded close to their father that they should not take a lesson from Daddy, while Herbert proudly pinned his blue ribbon to his lapel for all to see.

Clemmie felt exuberant with how marvelously the outing had gone, and in her glee she squeezed Joel's arm. "I can't tell you when I've had such a delightful day," she said as they walked among the booths again. "Being here with you as my escort has been the highlight of my week, no, make that my year!"

He lifted his eyebrows in surprise. "You must lead a very dull life."

She couldn't help the laugh that escaped. "Hardly dull—"

"Joel Litton, is that you?" a woman's voice exclaimed in surprise.

Clemmie felt her balloon of mirth deflate and her heart

drop to her stomach as a young woman with light brown hair and sea green eyes, as beautiful as any movie star in Hannah's memorabilia photo box, glided their way. She reminded Clemmie of a cross between Jennifer Jones and Lana Turner, with both an exotic innocence and cool sophistication.

Instantly Clemmie didn't like her.

"It's Paisley Wallace," the woman said to Joel. "We met at my sister's party when you first moved to Connecticut. My great-uncle owns the newspaper where Herbert works."

"Oh yes. How are you, Paisley?"

"I'm fine. I—I hope you're well," she said, clearly not knowing what to say.

Joel motioned with his cane. "As you can see. . ."

The girl's classic features softened in sorrow. "No, I—I didn't know. We didn't even know you were back in town. Sheridan will be pleased to learn of it. You just so suddenly disappeared. . . ."

"Perhaps, under the circumstances, it would be best not to tell her."

"Oh. Of course." Paisley glanced toward Clemmie, noticing her arm linked around Joel's. Clearly flustered, she made a few trite comments about the fair and the weather before excusing herself, while Clemmie jealously wondered who Sheridan was and what kind of hold she'd had on Joel.

"Shall we continue?" Joel suggested, his voice losing its earlier spark.

The rest of the day passed with an uncomfortable wall of reserve between them, which resulted in the adults trying to force the ease they'd earlier enjoyed. Their attempts made the atmosphere more taut. The children continued to frolic along the fairgrounds like excited puppies, oblivious to the changes.

"So," Joel said when they were alone, once Herbert and Thea excused themselves to take both girls to enjoy a nearby attraction of a pony ride. "Tell me your last name."

eleven

"Wh–what?"

He noticed how her voice trembled.

"Your last name. We were interrupted before."

"My name?" Her voice rose higher in pitch, but that could have been because of a noisy crowd of children who ran past. "Is it so important?"

Why was she evading the subject? "I'd like to know."

"I'm not sure why—"

"Are you going to make me guess?" he asked incredulously.

"If you like."

He shook his head, flabbergasted that she should take his joking seriously. A previous thought occurred to him.

"If we'd met somewhere before, you'd tell me, right?"

Another pause. "Of course." Her voice seemed tight, and he wondered if his question offended her.

"So is this a tale similar to Rumpelstiltskin, with you making me have to guess your name?"

She laughed in delight. "Oh, I haven't heard that tale in ages! It was in a book my mother read to me as a child. My favorite story was 'Rapunzel.' She was locked up in a stone tower by a cruel man so that her true love couldn't reach her. But he always found a way to her side by climbing her thick rope of hair. I used to envy her beautiful, long, golden hair. . . ."

What's the matter, Carrottop?

Stop it, Joel! I hate my hair! Why'd I have to have ugly orange hair anyway? I wish I could be Rapunzel and have her pretty, long, golden hair.

Aw, don't feel so bad. It's not that orange. . . .

"Joel. . . ? Are you all right?"

Marielle's concern shook him from an old memory of a

94

girl who'd been like a kid sister to him at the farm. "Yeah, fine. But you're changing the subject."

"Can't we have this discussion later?"

Again he shook his head in baffled surprise. "It's just a name, for crying out loud. Not your entire history."

"But that comes next, right?"

He couldn't understand her strange defensiveness and reluctance to talk about herself. "Okay, I'll admit I am interested in knowing more about you. But for now I just want a name."

"And I told you, I'll tell you that and everything else—later. Right now I just want to enjoy the rest of this day."

He tightened his hand around her arm to stop her from walking farther. "You're upset. Why? Is the prospect of telling me your full name so earthshaking? Are you a fugitive hiding from the law?"

"No, of course not. I just. . . Who's Sheridan?"

"Sheridan?" His mouth parted in surprise that she would ask such a question. "A woman I took out a few times. Why?"

"I just wondered."

This entire conversation perplexed him. This woman perplexed him.

He remembered a conversation he and Herbert once had. His friend had just had an argument with his wife, and he and Joel discussed women and their bizarre mood swings that made little sense—they were so hard to figure out!

But with each day that passed, Joel found himself wanting to figure out this woman and very badly. To focus on another person after a year of thinking only of himself was oddly. . .freeing. He'd been selfish; he knew that. At the time he hadn't cared, had been able to concentrate only on his bitterness and anger. But today he'd not only stepped out of the safe box of his home into the big, bad, wide world, but out of the cage that had enclosed his heart from feeling. To feel had been too painful. It was still painful. But now he had reason to try.

She was that reason.

It was foolish, it was crazy, perhaps even impossible as he'd told her before. But she hadn't pulled away from him every time he told her she should, instead always reaching out to him. And as unbelievable as it seemed, she sounded jealous when speaking of Sheridan. He resolved to test his theory at the next available moment when they were alone.

Soon, but not soon enough for Joel, the children complained of being tired. As the sun dipped low—the coolness of the air a testimony to evening's arrival—they decided to call it a day.

The drive back was quiet. Marielle's body relaxed against his, and he wondered if she had dozed off. His assumption proved correct when her silky hair brushed his jaw as her head slowly nodded off until it dropped to his shoulder. An unexpected surge of protection shot through him along with the sudden desire to hold her, but he resisted the temptation. She jerked awake, her warmth immediately absent as she quickly lifted her head. He heard her hands rapidly smooth her skirts, as if flustered, but neither of them spoke until they reached Herbert's home.

"Come talk to me?" he asked.

He sensed her sudden tension. "Can it wait? I'm really very tired and don't feel much like talking."

"It won't take long."

"Joel. . ."

"I'm not asking for personal disclosures. Not tonight anyway. Please?" He hadn't used that word in ages, not without sarcasm, and recognized her surprise in the shaky breath she inhaled.

"All right."

Marielle asked the chauffeur to wait and walked with Joel toward his shed. Though she didn't take his arm and he didn't take hers now that he was on familiar territory, he could sense her mounting anxiety.

"Relax," he murmured when they reached his porch. "I just have a favor to ask."

"I can't guarantee anything. It depends on the favor."

He turned to face her. "I want to see you, Marielle. Will

you let me do that?"

"See me?" she asked, clearly puzzled. "How?"

"Like this."

And he lifted his hands, gently pressing his fingertips to her smooth jaw.

❧

Clemmie trembled at his unexpected touch. Any lethargy she felt disappeared in an instant as her blood pounded like a living thing, making her head swim.

"Do you mind?" he whispered, not taking his hands away.

She couldn't speak, only shook her head the barest fraction in consent.

His fingertips continued along her jawline, warm and gentle. He moved his hands higher, his fingers flush against her cheeks, their tips learning her cheekbones. Higher still and she closed her eyes as his touch ghosted along her lashes and eyelids, gently swept her brows and temples, and trailed upward to brush her forehead. He moved them into her thick hair, weaving through the strands, and then his large hands cupped her scalp and swept down over her ears, to the ends of her wavy hair, down to her shoulders. . .sweeping above her collar to brush slowly upward again. . .along her neck. . . beneath her chin.

Clemmie shivered strongly but not from chill. Warmth rushed through her when his fingertips slowly drifted feather light across her lips.

"What. . .what are you doing to me?" he whispered, his breath suddenly warm against her mouth. "Don't you know this isn't possible?"

"No, no I don't—"

And suddenly his lips covered her own, cutting off her adamant whisper.

Being kissed once by Joel had been an unattainable dream come true, a momentary wish fulfilled that just as soon ended.

Being kissed twice brought the dream into startling reality, no longer unattainable, this kiss no fleeting reminder.

Just as his hands learned her face, his mouth took time making its own discoveries. Barely able to stand, she wound her arms around his neck, soon returning his kiss with eagerness.

After a long moment of bliss, he drew back and pressed his forehead to hers. She felt so lightheaded she continued to cling to him for support. Gradually her eyes fluttered open, looking into his beautiful, unseeing ones, taking in his perfect features and stunned expression as they both caught their breath.

"I...I should go," she whispered at last.

"Yes." His agreement came quiet.

"I'll come back tomorrow," she said needlessly, pulling her arms away from him and stepping back, contrary to what she truly wanted: to wrap her arms tightly around him again, melt in his warm embrace, and share in another heart-escalating kiss.

If things were complicated before, they'd just reached a point of total insanity.

She hugged herself, feeling suddenly chilled as she hurried from his porch and toward the house. Before she entered Thea's kitchen, she glanced over her shoulder and noticed Joel hadn't changed position or moved from his spot.

She burst inside, finding Thea at the stove, and fell into the closest chair.

"Dear God in heaven, help me," she whispered in a plea, her elbows on the table, her face in her hands. "I love him. I've never stopped—"

"I know."

"You *know*?" Clemmie peeked up through her fingers.

"Everyone who has eyes does. It's been as clear as a summer's day."

Clemmie realized she'd only fooled herself into believing otherwise. "This isn't some girlhood crush anymore, Thea. It's escalated into something much stronger, much dearer. He means everything to me! I can't imagine a day without him. I think my heart would drain empty because he has everything inside. . . . Oh, what am I going to do? I have to tell him the truth, I have no choice anymore. He's starting to question me. At the fair I evaded him, but I think he might suspect something's amiss with my crazy answers and the way I avoided giving him the answer he wanted. When he finds out who I am, what if he's not angry? What if he's disappointed—to learn it's me? The clumsy little carrottop he once knew? That's what he called me, you know. I can't hold a candle to the beauties he's been involved with. And I can't bear his rejection, which is sure to come."

"You don't give yourself enough credit. You have many fine qualities."

"You mean besides deception and fraud?" she wryly asked. "Oh, I should have never done this. You were right. I've made such a mess of things."

Thea came to her side and put a hand on her shoulder to calm her. "It's impossible to second guess what'll happen once Joel knows. But whatever does happen, please remember I'm here if you need me. And, Clemmie? You must tell him soon. Tomorrow. Better yet, go back there and tell him now."

"Now? No! I can't. N—not after. . ." She trailed off, thinking of his kiss, that wondrous moment she wasn't willing to share. "Tomorrow?" The prospect made her heart race. "It's too soon. I—I need more time."

"You've had more than enough time. I watched you two together today. You've gained his trust, and things are finally on an even keel between you. There's no longer any reason to hold back in telling him who you are."

There were plenty of reasons! Had Thea not heard anything Clemmie told her?

Feeling as if she were suffocating and in need of air, she shot up from the chair. "I—I have to go now. I'm sorry."

"Wait!" Thea called after her.

But she was already out the door and hurrying to the waiting chauffeur.

"Henley, please take me home."

He nodded, shutting the car door behind her, and hurried to resume his place at the wheel. All through the drive back to the mansion, the knowledge of what she must do haunted Clemmie. Upon arriving, she found no one home, and relieved she hurried to her room. But simply closing the door couldn't block out what must be done.

She had to tell him the next time she saw him. . . .

Tomorrow.

The word crashed like a brass gong, booming out a sentence of judgment in her mind.

twelve

Clemmie took a deep breath and knocked, equipped with her sweet peace offering that she hoped would make the bitter pill of what Joel must soon swallow easier to bear.

"It's open."

His voice sounded grim, and once she stepped inside, she noticed his expression matched his tone. Wonderful. He was in one of his dark, brooding moods. Perhaps it would be best to wait with personal declarations of guilt. . . .

Relieved that she had evaded her unwanted mission for one more day, she moved to stand before him where he sat in a chair.

"I brought you a treat," she said cheerily, hoping to dispel his gloom. "I baked it fresh this morning. That's why I'm late."

"Really."

"Yes." She set the pan down and removed the towel cover. "I think you'll like it."

"Because you know so much about me."

"Well, yes. I'm learning."

"From all those stories Herbert had to tell."

Uneasy, she studied his expression. He may as well have been wearing a mask; his face gave nothing away.

"Well, that, too. But I feel I've gotten to know you for myself."

"And that's important, isn't it? Getting to know me."

Clemmie swallowed hard, his pointed questions making her nervous.

"It helps."

"Yet I know nothing about you."

"I told you I'll tell you all you want to know soon."

"Soon. Right." He laughed harshly then frowned. "Forget soon. Tell me now."

She cut a hunk of the bread. "Not when you're like this. Later."

"It's always later with you, isn't it?"

She handed him a slice. "Here. Maybe this will help sweeten that nasty disposition of yours."

He snatched the bread from her hand with a frown and took a bite. His scowl grew darker. To her shock, he threw the rest of the bread on the table. His eyes were blind, but they sparked with blue flames as they snapped her way.

Wishing only to escape, she retreated a step. "I—I think I left something at Thea's. I'll be back shortly."

His hand flew to her arm, securing her. "You're not going anywhere. . .Clemmie."

At his mocking twist on her name and the knowledge that he knew it, she felt faint. She pressed her other palm flat to the table to steady herself.

"W–why did you call me that?" she whispered.

"Do you deny it's your name?"

She didn't answer, wishing for escape and knowing there wasn't any.

"You really must take me for a fool. There were so many pieces that didn't add up. Your refusal to talk about yourself, some of the bizarre things you said, your vague description of your appearance. But this—" The hand not clamped around her arm found the bread he'd tossed and raised it. "This was the dead giveaway. You should have been more careful, Clemmie. Darcy's date nut bread is one of a kind, like no one else's."

"S–so it was the bread?" she nervously asked. "That recipe could belong to anyone. Maybe Darcy gave it to Thea, and she gave it to me."

"Still trying to deny it?" he bit out. "Don't bother. I heard the tail end of the conversation you had with Thea last night. Through the kitchen window. I actually left my porch to find Herbert and got the unpleasant shock that you were withholding your identity from me. Adding it all together, it didn't take long to figure out, *Clementine Lyons*."

"All right"—she gave in, almost shouting the words—"all right, Joel. You caught me. And you may not believe this, but I'm really sorry it had to be this way. You don't know how sorry! But you gave me no choice." Her own temper rising, Clemmie wrenched her arm from Joel's hold. "If you hadn't concealed your whereabouts—if you'd only called or written us one time in these past three years—I wouldn't have felt the need to deceive you!"

He blinked in surprise, clearly not expecting an attack. "You're not actually turning this around on me, are you?"

"You're just as much to blame as I am! Yes, I was wrong to keep my identity secret—I admit it. All I wanted to do—all I ever wanted to do—was help you! But your pride is too big for your fool head. Otherwise you might have realized there are those who care about you and support you and would have helped if only you'd asked. But no, you didn't stop to consider that we might be concerned by your sudden disappearance, with no explanations, no word, not even one lousy letter. And heaven help me, I have no idea why we care so much, but we do. My parents love you. I love you. And—"

Clemmie broke off her spiel when she realized what she'd just admitted. Her mouth dropped open at her slip, her face flaming with humiliation. She whirled around and fled out the door.

In shock, she heard his steps pound behind her, closing in on her, right before he grabbed her waist. His other hand then found her arm, and he spun her around to face him. "Oh no, Clemmie. You're not getting away that easy." He grabbed both her arms, and she thought he might shake her. "I want some answers. And I won't take 'later' or 'soon' this time!"

He towered over her, so close that on the overcast day she could see within his sky blue eyes the fascinating kaleidoscope of darker blue that rimmed his irises. How had he moved, even over familiar territory, so swiftly and accurately, like a wildcat pouncing on its prey? He'd lost none of his agility, none of his enthralling power that made her go weak every time he was near. If anything, those traits had become enhanced through his adversity.

Breathless, she stared up at him, feeling as lightheaded as she'd been when he kissed her. And she wanted that again, wanted desperately to feel his lips claim hers and his strong arms enfold her against him. Something painful twisted inside her heart when she realized that would never happen again.

"You want answers, Joel? All right." She forced her voice to calm. "I would never have felt the need to deceive you had you behaved like a civilized human being instead of some rude, unmannerly, uncouth beast when I first came here. I didn't know you were here, not originally. I came to visit Hannah Thomas for the summer and paid Thea a visit. It was all a matter of happenstance that we met. But I knew if I told you who I was, you wouldn't have listened to a word I had to say. You would have just been angry that I'd found you and learned your secret. Tell me that's not true."

He didn't bother denying it.

"I thought so. Perhaps my methods were wrong, but my motive was pure. I wanted to show you that you weren't alone in this world and try to help you find a reason to live again. I had hoped I might convince you to have the operation, to call my parents—"

His mouth thinning, he released her and in so doing pushed her back.

"And that's the problem right there! You keep pushing away the people who care about you. As Clemmie, I wouldn't have had a chance, but as Marielle, a stranger working for you, you might have listened to me. You *did* listen to me."

Tears of angry frustration clouded her vision and leaked down her cheeks. "No one thinks you're your father's son. You're not a con artist anymore or a thief. Sometimes a person needs help, and I know my parents would gladly pay for any operation you need. They're proud of you and think of you as their own flesh and blood, their son. They love all the boys at the refuge, but you've always had a special place in their hearts because you're one of the originals, because you've come so far. Mother told me so. They would dearly love to help if you would only ask them."

"Leave it alone, Clemmie," he said gruffly, taking a brisk step from her. "Just go back home and leave me alone."

"There. There it is. Now you have your reason. And you've just proven every word I said is true." She kept her head held high, though she wanted to sink to the ground in misery. "Maybe what I did was wrong, but at least before you knew I was Clemmie and rejected me—as I knew you would, as you've just done—at least for a short time you emerged from this box of a home you've turned into a prison. At least you had one small taste of what it felt like to really live again. And it's up to you now if you're going to live on that little taste from this day forward or if you're going to take another step away from your cage and decide one small taste just wasn't enough. I really hope you make the right choice."

Her heart aching, she left him standing there. As Clemmie approached the back porch, Thea opened the screen door, her expression sympathetic. Inside the kitchen, Clemmie allowed her trembling bravado to splinter, and she collapsed in tears against her friend.

"He knows," she whispered between shaking sobs. "A—and he hates me. I've ruined everything. Oh, God, help me. H–him. Us. Please help us." She whispered the prayer against Thea's shoulder. "What have I done?"

ぇ

Joel stomped back to the shed, the path so familiar he didn't need to count steps, though even with all the noise Clemmie made when running from him, he was surprised he'd caught her so easily, as if attuned to her every movement, even if he couldn't see them.

Moving through the door he'd left open, he frowned at the thought of entombing himself within these four walls another day. Blast the girl, she had made what he once regarded his sanctuary feel like the prison she'd called it. It didn't help that a trace of her lilac scent always lingered in the air, no matter how many hours since she'd left or how long he kept the door open to try to remove the reminder of her. The second chair at his table also bore silent testimony to her frequent presence in his home, as if she belonged there.

Strangely, without her presence, his home didn't feel. . . complete.

With a grimace, he thought about removing the chair to the porch, but as he let his fingers trail the table to guide him, they bumped against two books she'd left behind in her haste. The smaller one on top was undoubtedly the novel she'd been reading to him, and the thick, larger one beneath with the thin, rough leather cover. . .it didn't take two guesses to know its identity.

Nor could he ignore the dull ache in his chest that never went away, the need to reach out again to a God who couldn't want anything to do with him any longer. Not after his long record of mistake after mistake, each worse than the last. He was serving the penalty for his crimes, he knew that. At times he railed at God—when the pain and despair threatened to choke him—but deep down, Joel knew he was solely to blame.

He'd been resigned to living out his purgatory on earth, but then she had come charging into his life—with her broom, dusters, and maddening doggedness.

Joel growled, shoving the books away. When he first realized her deception, he'd been furious and impatient to confront her. Now, after challenging his saintly tormentor, her words exasperated him no end.

Granted, he was wrong to have kept news of his whereabouts from the couple who'd raised him. It seemed like the best idea at the time, but he hadn't realized they'd be worried. They had so many children to look after, all with checkered pasts, he didn't think once he left their home to strike out on his own they would give him more than a fleeting thought.

And then there was Clemmie. . . .

He still worked to reconcile the woman he'd known as Marielle with the young girl he'd last seen at the refuge. There had been hints in the past weeks; he could see that now: the British phrases she sometimes used, so much like her mother's and Darcy's; her favorite story; even her familiarity with him from the start and her bossiness that daily combated a sweet nature. . . Yes, he could see Clemmie now in everything she'd done. But he could also see the woman she'd become, because it was that woman he had come to know.

And she had told him she loved him.

It hadn't been difficult to see her infatuation with him when she was a child, and he wondered if she still felt that same little-girl adoration. But how could she? He had been worse than an ogre, had rarely said one kind thing to her since she'd found him. A childish fascination would have quickly crumbled in the reality of all the cruel things he'd said and done.

He was still angry with her, but as the minutes passed, he grew calmer, remembering all she'd said to him, the reasons she'd given for her ruse. And she'd been correct; he would have sent her packing the moment he learned the truth.

But something had happened since then. . . .

She had felt familiar to him from the start, soon making him feel at ease where no other woman had, especially since the accident. As a child, she'd done the same. A bond of friendship had formed between them, despite their age difference, and he didn't have to pretend to be someone he wasn't around her. His chums at the refuge had looked up to him, making it impossible to confide in them when he felt in the doldrums, since they'd regarded him as a leader who couldn't fail. And that was part of the problem. His accursed pride made it impossible to contact anyone at the farm with news of what he'd become. A blind sinner. Clemmie may have hero-worshipped him as a little girl. . .but she'd also been genuine, letting him be who he truly was.

And she had not changed as a young woman.

The walk to Herbert's house wasn't familiar to Joel, so he counted steps, knowing Herbert kept the level ground free of debris. As long as that wretched cat didn't run across his path, he would have no problems.

He heard the women's voices through the kitchen window Thea had left open and felt reassured he wasn't too late. He knocked twice in warning then opened the kitchen door. A hush settled over the room, Clemmie's subdued sniffling the only sound.

"I'll just go check in on Loretta," Thea said, her steps hurrying from the room.

Joel appreciated her effort to give them privacy but didn't want to risk any chance of being overheard. "You and I need to talk."

"Look. . . ." Clemmie's voice trembled. "I know I was wrong, and I'm sorry. A thousand times over, I'm sorry. I'm not sure what else you want me to say, except I hope one day you can forgive me for—"

He put up a hand to silence her.

"Will you come outside with me?" He sensed her hesitation. "You had your turn to speak. Now there's something I need to say."

He thought she might never answer. "A–all right."

He heard the rustle of her skirt and the slight skid of the chair on the floor. He waited until she approached then stepped aside to let her precede him.

thirteen

"There should be an apple tree beyond the shed. With a tire swing for the girls. Herbert told me about it."

Clemmie blinked in stunned amazement. Talk of apple trees was the last thing she'd expected Joel to say. "Yes?"

"Guide me there."

She swallowed hard, grateful he couldn't see her damp cheeks. Was Joel actually asking for assistance? Gingerly taking his arm, she walked with him to the tree, not far from the edge of the woods. His hand went to the trunk, familiarizing himself with where he was, and he sank to the ground.

Clemmie remained standing and stared, openmouthed.

"Won't you join me? I seem to remember you had a fondness for the outdoors and didn't mind getting your clothes dirty."

"I didn't, when I was a little girl." Regardless, she sank beside him on the dry grass, sitting on her legs. "Joel, what's this about?"

His sightless blue eyes seemed to stare at the horizon, his expression undergoing a swift change. He looked very sad, and Clemmie held her breath.

"When I was in the service, I made friends with another sailor in my unit whose term ended the same time as mine. His father owned a lumber company, and he convinced me to get a job with him when our time was up."

Clemmie listened, her eyes wide. Joel was talking to her? Did this mean he'd forgiven her?

"Things went well for a while; then his father lost the company. In that time, I'd. . .well, I met up with some people—friends of Jim's—and got into some trouble." He sighed. "I'm not going about this very well, am I? I've never told anyone all of it, not even Herbert."

Clemmie's amazement grew. He'd chosen to *confide* in her?

"I started gambling. Heavily. Drinking. Carousing in town with the fellows. Used up most of my income. Jim did, too. He met a girl he fell hard for, wanted to marry her and live the honest life—and I kept pushing him to go on our wild binges. The accident was my fault. The weekend before his wedding, I convinced him to do one more night on the town. She didn't want him to. He held back, but I persisted till he gave in. Him and two of our pals. . ." His words came bitter, low. Tears filmed his eyes. "I wish to God that He would let me live that night over! That I could go back and change everything. . ."

Clemmie held her hand hard in an effort not to touch him in comfort. She sensed he needed physical distance in order to say what had been burdening his heart for over a year.

"I had cracked a joke—you know me, funny man Joel—and he looked away from the road. At me. I still remember him laughing. A deer ran in front of the car. One of the guys cried out a warning. Jim swerved and went over an embankment. That's the last I remember seeing any of them. I woke up in a hospital and learned my friends all died in the crash. I got thrown from the car but have no idea how I survived."

Clemmie's heart felt ripped in two by his pain. Something occurred to her. "Oh, but Joel, you know it wasn't your fault, don't you—"

He put up a hand to silence her.

"After I was released from the hospital, I visited his mother to express my regrets. I learned his fiancée tried to overdose. It seems she was pregnant with his kid. They admitted her to a mental facility to get help. She lost the baby."

Clemmie could scarcely breathe from the painful pressure in her chest. Oh, so much made sense now! So much. . .

"That's why you didn't go through with the operation," she whispered. "It wasn't just about money, about asking my parents for help. You didn't feel you deserved it."

"All of it, Clemmie—all of it was my fault. From the start.

I didn't want your parents to know what kind of man I'd become and be ashamed and sorry they ever knew me. I've failed so much in life—I didn't want them to know I'd done it again. I felt this was God's punishment. That's a big part of why I didn't pursue an operation. I felt I didn't have the right to see when others had died. So now you know. And now you can understand why I can't do it."

Glad he couldn't see the tears that ran down her cheeks, she worked to keep her voice even. "Joel, that's not God's way. He wouldn't hurt you like that. You're not to blame! You can't help it that a deer ran across the road or that your friend wasn't paying attention at that precise moment. No more than my mother could help it when she found herself trapped in a relationship with an abusive con man who forced her to assist him in taking Lady Annabelle's necklace on the *Titanic*. No more than Darcy could help it when she was a lost little girl fending for herself in London's streets and doing anything she could to survive, even if that meant stealing."

"Ah, but there's a difference, Clemmie." His tone came wry. "They didn't know better. I did. And your mother was trying to protect her life."

"I still say, God isn't like that. He doesn't want you to suffer, to make your own penance by living in a box, refusing the chance to see again. You're repentant for your actions. God can and will and does forgive you, Joel—but will you forgive yourself?"

"What right do I have to see, when Jim's mother will never have her son back?"

"Does she blame you for the accident?"

He grew quiet. "No."

"Then why should you?"

At her soft words, he heaved a weary sigh. "There were others—"

"Grown men with the ability to make their own choices. And the woman, his fiancée. . .if she would try something so horrible as that, who's to say she didn't already have considerable problems?"

The slightest smile tugged the corners of his mouth. "You sound like your mother."

"Is that a bad thing?"

"I'll get back to you on that."

She smiled through her tears. Not exactly a reassurance but his old teasing manner suggested there would be future encounters between them, allowing the light of her dream to flicker again.

However it had happened, whatever his reasons, Joel had reconciled with her.

She wouldn't ask for explanations; she would thank God for His merciful hand that had once again intervened to mend the outcome of her own foolish mistakes.

❧

"Out twice in one week?" Herbert's voice shocked Joel who'd been so absorbed in trying to fasten his tie he hadn't heard his steps creak on the porch. "That's one for Guinness, isn't it?"

"Will you just help me tie this blasted thing?" Joel whipped the ends from the mangled mess of the knot he could feel with his fingertips. He hadn't worn a tie in over a year. Even with sight, he'd been lousy in the art of knotting one.

"I'm not much better, but I'll give it a go." Herbert's steps came closer. He took the ends from Joel's hands and began the intricate steps of the accursed rite that polite society demanded. "So what's the occasion for the glad rags? I'd forgotten you owned anything so nifty."

"The bazaar." Joel said the words as if it was an execution chamber.

"Oh that. You're going?"

"You're not?"

"Duty calls, old boy. I must head to the newspaper office. I was just coming by to see if you needed anything." He tugged the tie sharply, pushing the knot up to Joel's neck. "Clemmie talk you into it?"

"I can't believe she did. Again."

Herbert chuckled. "You're just putty in her hands."

Joel shoved Herbert's hands away and made the final adjustment himself. "That's not funny."

"Oh, so you're not?" Herbert made a disbelieving sound in his throat. "That gal has had you wound around her little finger ever since she was old enough to say your name— before that even. Now it's worse."

"You're all wet," Joel grumbled. "You have no idea what you're gabbing about."

"No? All of us were sure you'd shoot through the roof once you learned the truth. Not only did you not barricade yourself inside and refuse to see her again—you did the exact opposite. Actually left your porch, went off somewhere with her for a good half hour, and came back as friends. Don't get me wrong—I think it's great you recovered so fast. But it's not what we expected."

"I was angry at first, sure. Who wouldn't be? But to realize it was Clemmie, that someone from the past cared enough to do something like that. . . It didn't bother me like I thought it might. Besides, what right do I have to hold a grudge after all the grief I've caused others?"

"My, my," Herbert said in awe. "Clemmie must be a miracle worker for you to talk like that. Joel Litton: sinner turned saint."

Joel grunted. "Will you knock it off? I'm hardly a saint."

"Hmm. Offer still stands, you know. The one I've issued again and again. Now that you're out and about and have no excuses, come with us to church Sunday."

"Clemmie asked me, too." Joel grew somber. "I can't see how God would want me in His house after all this time."

"Well, that's where *you're* all wet."

"Yeah, maybe, but not in the way you mean. I burned my bridges when I turned my back on Him."

"Did you? Turned your back completely? I don't think so. There's a sadness in your voice when you say that, Joel. . .

Remember what Darcy used to tell us: 'There isn't a bridge God can't rebuild, if you'll let Him be the carpenter.'"

"Actually she said 'ain't a bridge.'"

"And Brent winced every time she used bad grammar or her cockney accent."

Herbert's reminder caused Joel to crack a smile. "They did make an odd sort of couple."

"Speaking of couples. . ."

"Don't say it," Joel warned, sensing what was coming.

"You two make a nifty one."

Joel sighed. "I'm blind."

"Whether you can or can't see doesn't seem to make one bit of difference in Clemmie wanting to be with you."

"There is the age difference. Twelve years."

"She's not a kid anymore. Unless age is a problem for you."

"Just drop it." It wasn't a problem; he'd known her age when he first kissed her—just not that she was Clemmie. At first it felt odd to realize the girl he'd considered a kid sister was the young woman he'd kissed and who had made him feel emotions deeper than he'd known before. But because of all his present obstacles, Joel had not given much thought to developing a romantic relationship. He held his arms out to the sides. "Will I pass?"

"Hmm. Well, if the fashionable new look for society is one brown sock and one black, you look swell."

"Funny." Joel didn't take him seriously, since he owned only one color.

A light step on the porch followed by the sudden aroma of lilacs alerted him to her presence.

"Joel. . . ?"

Strange that his breath should come short and his heart so suddenly clench at the sound of her soft, husky voice, when he'd heard it for weeks.

He turned to face her, and she gave a little gasp.

fourteen

"Is something wrong?" Joel asked.

"Wrong?" Clemmie worked to keep her voice natural. The sudden sight of him always took her breath away, but she really had to get a grip on her emotions. "Nothing's wrong. I came a little early. I hope that's all right. I can wait on the porch."

"No need. We're done here." Joel's face gave nothing away, and she wondered what the two men had been discussing. She had the oddest feeling the subject had been her.

Herbert smiled. "I need to get to work. Have fun at the bazaar."

"Hannah's mother lent her chauffeur again if you'd like us to give you a lift."

"I enjoy the walk. Helps clear my head. Thanks all the same, Clemmie."

Once Herbert left, her footsteps moved farther into the shed. "You look very nice."

Joel's answering smile was grim. "I wish I could offer you the same compliment."

Oh no! He isn't in another of his black moods again, is he?

Quickly she closed the distance. "I brought you something. Take a seat."

"Is there time?"

"I told you I came a little early." She pushed the cigar box into his hands. "Do you remember this?"

A puzzled expression crossed his handsome features. He lifted the wooden lid, his fingertips warily searching the interior. A delighted smile suddenly flashed across his face, causing Clemmie to haul in another swift intake of breath at the pleasant change it made to his entire being.

115

"My boyhood treasures!" He withdrew an iridescent blue black feather of a jay, his forefinger tracing its soft edge. "You kept it all this time?" His tone came wondering.

"Of course. You asked me to keep it safe before you left for the service. Since you know who I am now, I thought you should have it back."

His smile faded into gentle melancholy. "Thank you, Clemmie. I don't know what to say."

She stared in wonder, noting moisture filmed his eyes. Never had she thought her return of his trinkets would affect him so deeply. She wished now she'd brought them earlier in the week, at a time when she and Joel didn't have to be anywhere and he could spend as much time reminiscing as he liked. But she'd promised Hannah she would attend and didn't want to disappoint her friend either.

"We should probably leave soon," she said reluctantly.

"Of course." His smile disappeared as he set the box on the table.

"You really don't want to do this, do you?"

"Can you blame me?"

"You survived the fair. Even enjoyed it."

"Yes, among strangers and those who already knew—of this." He motioned to his eyes with an impatient jerk of his hand.

"Hannah knows. And her mother. They don't think any less of you."

"They haven't seen me yet. It's bound to be awkward."

Clemmie hissed an annoyed breath. Talk about awkward! Sometimes he could be so difficult.

"If your present condition bothers you so much, you should have the operation."

"I told you why I can't."

"And I told you why that's rubbish. God doesn't want you to suffer, no more than any of us want you to suffer."

He shook his head in skepticism.

"Remember the thief on the cross? The one crucified next

to Jesus? That thief deserved punishment and suffering. But when he asked Jesus to remember him when He went to paradise, Jesus told the thief that he would be with Him that day. You've suffered, too, Joel. A great deal. And if you're bound and determined to believe that you deserve to carry out some crazy penance for what happened to your friends, well then, I should think that penance is long over and you've paid your debt in full. Now it's time to forget the past and turn back to God. He's never forgotten you."

Unable to bear another negative response, she moved out onto the porch to wait. No more than a minute passed before he joined her. He remained silent, his face a tense mask. But he took her arm, and together they went to the waiting car.

The ride remained silent, scrambling Clemmie's nerves, but she didn't dare speak. She didn't want further discord, and clearly Joel was upset with her.

The bazaar was crowded, held inside a huge room of a civic building Hannah's mother had rented, and Clemmie marveled that not one foot of unused space appeared visible. Everywhere—against the walls, in the center of the great room—stood antiques, knickknacks, useful and decorative objects, and some modern items as well. All of them were itemized, along with a description of their use neatly printed on each attached yellow tag—very helpful on some of the more unusual antiques, which at first glance had no purpose Clemmie could identify.

To a passing stranger, she and Joel might look like a couple in love, as close as they walked, but Clemmie knew better. For whatever reason, Joel had decided not to bring his cane, and he stuck to Clemmie like glue, holding her arm tightly. She made sure to point out each step or problem in the path that could hamper him.

They stopped walking with the crowd so Clemmie could inspect a cuckoo clock, something for which Darcy had often expressed a fondness, thinking the little bird that popped out "quite a corker."

"Clemmie!" Hannah practically squealed. "I thought you'd never come. Joel, hi." Her tone went shy and girlish as she looked his way. "You may not remember me, but I'm Hannah from the refuge. Bill and Sarah's daughter."

"Of course I remember you." He gave her a kind smile. "Though you were just a little thing before I left. Seems you've grown up, too."

Hannah giggled. If Joel could see the manner in which the cute brunette prettily blushed, Clemmie felt sure he wouldn't worry so about how others perceived him. Blind or with sight, Joel still had the ability to turn every young woman's head and make them act like little more than besotted schoolgirls. Had she been that bad as a child? With a flush of warmth, she realized she'd been worse, though she'd also been able to talk to him on a sensible level, not chattering away nervously as Hannah now did. Of course Hannah always had been a chatterbox.

"Mother will be so pleased to see you. What a surprise to learn you've lived here all this time. And, oh, you simply must come to the church picnic. They're holding it by the lake, and there will be croquet and plenty to eat and boating. . . ."

Sensing Joel withdraw at the mention of *church* just by the tensing of his muscles beneath her fingers, Clemmie was half-tempted to cover her free hand over her young friend's mouth. Instead she widened her eyes and raised her brows as a signal to stop. Hannah got the message.

"Oh, but just listen to me carrying on. I really should get back to work. Were you thinking of buying that cuckoo clock?"

"Yes. For Darcy. Her birthday is in two months. But I haven't decided. . . ." With regard to the benefit's good cause and the condition of the piece, the asked-for five dollars wasn't steep, but Clemmie didn't have much money left, not after buying the ingredients for Joel's special dinner, as well as a new hat and gloves for herself to wear to church. Her old ones had worn dreadfully, something sweet-but-blunt

Hannah had pointed out her first Sunday when she'd dressed for the church meeting.

"If it's for Darcy, I'm sure Mama would agree to knocking off a dollar or two. Darcy's always been such a lamb to us, and she helped Mama and Papa plenty when they first came from the island all those years ago."

"You're certain?"

"If there's a problem, I'll chip in the difference."

"Thank you, Hannah. You're a dear." Clemmie unsnapped her purse and pulled out three bills, which Hannah took with another smile at Joel then Clemmie, as if she approved.

Once Hannah left, Joel spoke. "Is there anything else you wanted to see?" To her surprise, he took the clock from her and tucked it under his free arm. Clearly he wanted to leave. Her mission accomplished, she longed for some place more quiet as well.

"No. We can go now."

His nod clearly relieved, they moved together toward the exit.

"Joel Litton, as I live and breathe," a sweet feminine voice said. A classy blond moved before him and put a light hand to his sleeve. He jerked, and Clemmie's gratitude that he hadn't dropped the clock barely eclipsed a surge of jealousy.

"Sheridan?"

She laughed brightly. "Yes, it's me. I'm glad you remember." She glanced at Clemmie, not one ounce of jealousy in her eyes, though Clemmie couldn't say the same for her own. "Hello, I'm Sheridan Wallace. An old friend of Joel's." She again looked at him. "Who's been a very naughty boy for not letting anyone know he was in town. Paisley told me, and when she did, I couldn't believe it. But here you are."

"Yes, here I am." Joel's voice sounded grim. "Did she also tell you I'm blind?"

Clemmie realized his condition might not be apparent, since he carried no cane.

No shock crossed Sheridan's elegant features. "She did."

Her manner became quiet and concerned. "And I'm very sorry to hear that happened to you, so very sorry. But tell me, where are you staying? Paisley mentioned you were with Herbert and his family. Surely you're not living there?"

She moved into the subject with such skill, making it clear she didn't consider his blindness a flaw. Clemmie wanted to hate her, just because of what the woman had once been to Joel, but found she couldn't bear such an immature grudge.

"Actually, I am." Joel's expression eased, and he smiled. "In his shed, if you can believe that."

Sheridan's big baby blues grew wider. "Oh, Joel, tell me you're not serious? Doesn't he have enough rooms in his house? I hate to think of you all alone in a cold shed with the spiders and rats—"

Joel laughed. "No rats. There are mice." His voice teased. "But it was my choice."

"But why? That's simply ridiculous."

Clemmie looked back and forth between them, feeling like an outsider watching a Ping-Pong match as they conversed. She thought Sheridan would never go away.

"I would love to stand here chatting all afternoon and catch up, but I have to get back. I've been on a break."

"You're working at the bazaar?" Clemmie asked in surprise.

"My mother is on the women's committee. Do you know Sarah Thomas? She runs it."

"She's my friend Hannah's mother. I'm staying with them for the summer."

"Really? My mother and her mother are best friends."

"Really?" Clemmie's tone lacked Sheridan's enthusiasm. "Small world."

"Isn't it? Listen, we simply must all get together sometime soon. Are you going to the church picnic next Sunday?"

"You go to their church, too?" Clemmie's heart dropped another level. "I've never seen you."

"We sit in the balcony."

"Oh."

"Well, if you'll be at the picnic, we must talk more then. I really have to go."

"I look forward to catching up," Joel said with a smile.

Clemmie gave him a sharp look, one which, of course, he couldn't see and she couldn't help. She practically bit her tongue in two so she wouldn't spout anything that might make her seem green-eyed with envy. Because, she realized with a grimace of self-loathing, that's exactly what she was.

❧

Clemmie remained quiet the entire drive back, and Joel wondered what bothered her. To try lighting the atmosphere, since he knew he'd brought about enough dark moods, he decided to share with her a decision he'd reached.

"Next Sunday, I'd like to go to church with you. Would you mind?"

She gasped. "Of course not, but after the way you acted before the bazaar, I, well. . .I must say I'm surprised. What changed your mind?"

He expected that question but not the tightness in her voice. Wasn't she pleased? She'd been bugging him for weeks to attend. "Between you and Herbert, I've been getting an earful. I guess something sank in. It doesn't mean I've changed my mind about everything, but I've been around crowds twice now and survived."

Actually those who knew him hadn't treated him much differently at all. Maybe at first he'd noticed a slight awkwardness and uncertainty about how to proceed because, he assumed, no one wanted to injure his feelings. On both occasions the discomfort had faded, if not disappeared altogether. And those he didn't know, well, he didn't really care what they thought. Clemmie had been right about that, too.

"Maybe I'm ready to take that next step," he added when she didn't respond.

"Then I'm honestly happy to hear it." Her tone became softer. "I'm sure you'll find it a lovely place. Since I've been there, I've found the people to be kind and caring. But we don't have to go to that picnic afterward if you don't want to."

"Would you rather we didn't?"

"No. It's just. . .I understand if you don't want to."

"I'll think about it."

He had hoped his answer would have eased the tension; instead, the resulting silence felt thicker than before.

fifteen

"I'm a terrible person, Hannah."

Her friend moved into view behind Clemmie, who stared soulfully at her image, trying to tame her wild waves with a comb. She gave up, dropping her arms to her sides.

"Why would you say such a thing?" Hannah's eyes were curious.

"Because it's true?" Clemmie slumped in the vanity chair. "This last week, Operation Save Joel has undergone significant improvement. He doesn't always give negative comebacks when I talk about his condition or suggest that he can enjoy life again. He's become more positive, nicer to be around."

"I must admit I agree from the little I saw of him. He's a real sheik! That man and the man you described to me after your first day there are poles apart! Still, I couldn't believe it when you told me he wanted to go to the church picnic. You've made remarkable progress!"

"Yes."

"So why so glum? You should be dancing for joy."

Clemmie gave a wry grin. "I question his motives for his sudden change of heart. Instead of accepting it at face value and being happy, I wonder if it's because of his old girlfriend. That's what makes me horrible."

Hannah put a hand to Clemmie's shoulder, looking at her in the mirror. "It doesn't make you horrible. It makes you human."

"If only she were mean and nasty, I wouldn't feel so bad."

"But she's not?"

"You tell me. You probably know her. Sheridan Wallace. Her mother is a friend of your mother's."

Hannah's eyes went huge. "Sheridan is Joel's old girlfriend?"

123

A sympathetic frown creased her brow. "Oh, yes. I can see your problem. She's tops. Very nice to everyone."

"Great," Clemmie said unenthusiastically. "You're a fan, too."

"Has Joel expressed. . .feelings for you?"

Clemmie hesitated. She couldn't tell her young friend about the kisses; they were too special to share, even with Hannah. "Nothing untoward or meaningful." On his part anyway.

"Oh good." Hannah's relief was evident. "Then I think you should just reflect on your reason for starting this whole endeavor. To help Joel learn to live again, which is exactly what you're doing."

Clemmie sighed. "You're right. I need to stop being selfish and do whatever I can to support and encourage him. Thank you for reminding me what truly matters. You're a real friend by keeping me in line. Don't take this wrong, but sometimes you seem so mature for your age."

"Mother would disagree. She doesn't like the girls I've been keeping company with, before you came. She says they're a bad influence and make me do childish things."

As Clemmie fastened her hat to her head, lowering the netting that covered the upper portion of her face, she wondered why she hadn't met them but didn't ask. She had enough to ponder.

Half an hour later, when she arrived at Herbert's, she found Joel in a pleasant mood, even offering cordial conversation to Hannah and her mother. Herbert had managed to get his car running, and he and his family followed in their Ford.

In church, Clemmie could feel Joel's tension—his body strained from where it touched hers in the crowded pew. Whether he got anything out of the message on releasing one's burdens to the Lord, she didn't know, but she felt it appropriate for his situation. They didn't spend time mingling afterward, instead driving straight to the picnic area.

"It's a beautiful day, isn't it?" he questioned almost sadly as they strolled, arm in arm, to a shady copse of trees. Today he'd brought his cane, but he still held fast to Clemmie's arm. "I can feel the warmth of the sun and smell the grass and flowers and even the water."

"You can smell water?" She knew his senses were sharpened but hadn't realized water had a smell.

"It's a cool, brisk scent. The grass is earthy but fresh. And the flowers. . ." He looked almost remorseful. "I wish I had paid more attention to the different kinds of wildflowers there are. I never cared much for them when I had my sight. They were all the same to me, except in color and shape of course. But a flower was a flower."

"Just as a rose is a rose by any other name."

An awkward silence ensued. Reminded of her duplicity, Clemmie hurried to add, "The ones we're walking among now are white and yellow. Some sort of daisies, perhaps?"

"I know the scent of roses," he answered her previous statement. "And lilacs. That's your scent. Soft and fresh. Brisk but soothing. . ."

Clemmie held her breath. Just what was he saying? Or was she reading too much into his low words?

"Joel!"

The breathless moment was disrupted as a newly familiar voice called his name. Clemmie turned to watch Sheridan's graceful approach. Even over uneven ground, she seemed to float.

"It's so wonderful to see you! I wasn't sure you were coming when we talked at the bazaar."

"I have persuasive friends."

"Oh?" Sheridan laughed and glanced at Clemmie. "Well, good for you! He can be so stubborn, can't he? Sometimes it takes a bulldozer to move him."

"Yes, he can be a cross between mule-headed and pigheaded."

"I'm here, too, ya know."

Clemmie smiled, ignoring his mock affront. "He's always been like that. We go far back. We were both children at the refuge. My parents ran the place."

"Oh! So you must be little Clemmie!" Sheridan's voice sounded pleased. "Joel told me all about you and growing up on the farm."

"Yes," she murmured, not thrilled to be referred to in such a manner.

"Clemmie and I have always been good friends."

She felt as if a weight dropped to her shoulders. By Joel's reply, of course Sheridan would understand they weren't dating. And they weren't, she reminded herself. So if he wanted to resume whatever relationship he had with the woman, Clemmie shouldn't feel betrayed.

She reminded herself of that all through the luncheon. Clemmie could barely eat the thin slice of pork—the pig donated by a wealthy church member—or the brown beans as she fought despondency. Sheridan stayed close to Joel, and given the manner in which they reminisced of past occurrences, Clemmie felt like a third wheel.

When Sheridan offered to get Joel a slab of peach pie, something else Clemmie knew he enjoyed, she gritted her teeth at the smile he gave the pretty blond, wishing his effusive thanks could have been for her instead. Indeed, he seemed quite in his element, his old gregarious nature for which he'd been greatly admired back in full strength.

Stop it, Clemmie! You're acting like a green-eyed witch, and you have no right. Just be happy he's happy. It's what you wanted.

Sheridan seemed not to notice Clemmie's tart responses to her questions or the little glares that she immediately tried to curb, and Clemmie did her best to improve her disposition, knowing it wasn't fair to either of them. But she couldn't help wishing more than once that Sheridan were a vindictive shrew and not the pleasant young woman who shared their company.

It was with great relief that Clemmie realized the picnic was coming to an end, as members of the congregation stacked dirty dishes in crates. Soon the blessed moment arrived when they made their farewells.

"It's been wonderful being with you today, Joel." Sheridan put her hand to his arm. "We really must do this again sometime. Do you still have my number?"

Clemmie wondered if her face had turned flame red due to the fire of jealousy building hotter inside.

"Not anymore, no."

"I'll give it to you."

"Won't do me much good. Can't read it, you know."

"Oh, but someone surely can read it to you if you ask. It would be better than me relying on that faulty memory of yours."

He laughed, and she joined in. Only Clemmie remained sober.

Equipped with Sheridan's number, which he'd stuffed inside his pocket, Joel walked with Clemmie to the waiting car. All through the drive back, Hannah happily chattered about a boy she'd met, but Clemmie wished for silence. Once the Rolls pulled into Herbert's drive, Joel took her hand, surprising her.

"Come with me inside Herbert's house. I have something I need to talk with you about."

"Oh, but. . ." Clemmie glanced at Hannah's mother, uncertain.

"We can send the chauffeur again," the woman assured. "Just give us a ring."

"Or Herbert could take her home, now that he has his car running," Joel assured. "Either way, you'll have a ride."

"All right."

She said a quick good-bye, sensing Joel wanted to speak before Herbert and his family returned. He'd taken them out for an ice cream soda to top off the day, a rare treat judging by the manner in which the girls had jumped up and down, squealing, when they heard his plan.

Joel used his cane to find the door and opened it for Clemmie. She preceded him inside, wondering what he had to say. She followed him to the sofa and sank beside him.

"Tell me before I burst, Joel. You're so mysterious. . . ."

"I guess I got that lesson from you," he teased.

"Joel . . . ," she warned.

"I've decided to have the operation."

sixteen

Clemmie grew so silent Joel could barely hear her breathe. He had thought she might squeal, like the girls often did, or display some other sign of enthusiasm since she'd been urging him for weeks to put the past behind him. Today at church, no, even before that with Clemmie, he'd begun to consider seriously the subject he'd chosen never to think of since his initial consultation with the doctor.

"Clemmie, did you hear me?" He twisted around and slid his hand on the cushion, leaning in her direction. The tips of his fingers suddenly met her hand, and she jerked back a little, as if scalded. He frowned, wondering why she acted so jumpy.

"Joel. . .I—I don't know what to say." Her voice trembled. "I'm so pleased you made this decision. Th–that you found something worthwhile to live for. . ."

Her words trailed off in a wistful fashion, and he drew his eyebrows together, confused. He moved his hand purposefully along the cushion until he found hers and covered it with his. "I wouldn't be where I am right now if it wasn't for you, Clemmie. You kept at me and wouldn't take no for an answer."

"Sometimes a stubborn will can be a blessing if you look hard enough. But only sometimes, Joel."

He chuckled. "That first part sounds like something Darcy might say."

"Actually, she did."

He heard the smile in her voice and laughed outright.

"And the last was a warning to me, hmm?"

"If you like." There was no mistaking the amusement in her voice.

He felt better now that the mysterious tension had eased but still found the next subject difficult to introduce. "Clemmie. . . about what you said regarding your parents and your grandfather. . .and. . .and helping me out—"

"Oh, they'd consider it a privilege!"

"What with these tough times we live in? And running the reformatory?"

"Grandfather's money is tied up in banks in England. My family wasn't affected like so many, and the refuge survives on the patronage of its investors. So you needn't worry, Joel."

She seemed so assured and confident Joel couldn't help but feel a spark of that same hope. "Well then, it seems I have a call to make. Would you mind getting things started?"

She gasped. "Oh—I'd love to. Are you sure Herbert won't mind?"

"He won't, and Clemmie, well, the charges will have to be reversed. I doubt Herbert could pay for the call, and I sure can't—"

Clemmie squealed as she jumped up from the sofa, keeping Joel's hand in hers and tugging him. "Oh that's no problem, I'm quite certain. Come on then! My parents will be thrilled to hear from you. I can't wait to tell them the good news— that you're here and alive. At times we did wonder. . . ."

Joel felt a niggling of guilt, again shocked that any of those at the refuge had given him more than a fleeting thought. He'd been such a troublemaker during the majority of his time there; he'd have thought they would feel relieved to have him out of their lives for good.

She led him down the hallway to where the phone was. He heard her connect with the operator and give the number of the refuge, asking to reverse the charges. It took awhile to get through, Clemmie's toe tapping almost wearing a hole through Joel's nerves, but at last she gave a delighted laugh.

"Aunt Darcy? Is that you? . . .Yes, it's me. I have some huge news to share, but you best be sitting down. . .no—no, nothing bad. Honest. . . Well, guess who's standing here beside me?" She took his hand in hers and gave it a squeeze. "It's Joel! He's here at Herbert's. . . . Yes, yes. . .all right."

Joel felt her prod him with the receiver. "She wants to talk with you."

Joel swallowed hard, fighting down the ridiculous impulse to cower or run. He felt like a boy reprimanded and sent to his guardian's office.

"Uh, hullo."

"Joel, bless me soul! As I live and breathe, it is you. What have you been doin' with yourself all these years, ye naughty boy? Why give us such a scare?"

Through the static it felt strangely good to hear Darcy's no-nonsense words chastise him in her distinctive British accent.

"It's a long story. I, uh, was hoping to speak with Mr. Lyons."

"Not before you explain yourself, young man. Where have you been?"

"Darcy, cease with all your fluttering and let the boy talk to Stewart." Even over the static, Joel heard Brent admonish his wife. Apparently they were both listening in.

"Uh, hi, Mr. Thomas." Nearly thirty years old, Joel still felt like a schoolboy talking with his teacher.

"Are you conducting yourself in an appropriate manner, Joel? You haven't blocked off any more pipes, have you?"

He laughed. Trust his old schoolmaster to say such a thing. And to remember when Joel had been the culprit behind climbing the roof and stuffing rags in the pipe of the old wood-burning stove, in the hope of getting a day free from schooling.

"No, sir. I've steered clear of all pipes."

"Good lad."

"Are you eating well?" Darcy wanted to know. "Are you getting enough to eat?"

Joel reassured her his health was fine; yes, his eating habits were normal, and yes, he really was alive and kicking. Soon

Clemmie's mom came onto the line, demanding to know all of what Darcy had already asked. Finally the phone was handed to Clemmie's father.

"Hello, sir." Joel squelched the emotion that coated his throat at the familiarity of hearing so many special voices from the past. "I actually called because I have a favor to ask."

His hand still in Clemmie's, he felt her give him an encouraging squeeze. As briefly as possible, he told his former guardian the basics of what had occurred and the reason for his call.

"Whatever you need, son," he said once Joel finished. "Just say the word. Do you remember when I first met you living in the streets, trying to con me by snagging my interest in that rigged shell game? Then that gentleman had you arrested for stealing from him, and I got the judge's permission to take you with me as one of my first boys to help at the refuge?"

Joel remembered; he'd been almost nine. He couldn't help the moisture that stung his eyes and closed them.

"I told you then that I didn't want you to think of me as just your guardian. That I wanted to be a father to you and would always be there when you needed me. You had only to ask."

"Yes, sir." The evidence of tears coated his voice, making it gruff.

"I meant it then, and I mean it now. Anything, Joel. We're family. You'll always be a son to me."

If he didn't get off this phone soon, he would humiliate himself by breaking down into a binge of weeping. He couldn't remember when he had last cried. "Yes, sir. Thank you, sir. This is only a loan. I'll pay back every penny."

"I know you will, though it's not necessary."

But it was to Joel. To clear his name of the criminal lifestyle his father had passed down to him, he was determined to stand on his own two feet, to prove that he could, and to never take another penny of charity.

Clemmie's father asked for details, and Joel answered as

best he could, explaining he hadn't yet been to see the doctor. The line filled with more static, the words fading out now and then and getting difficult to understand.

"Before we lose connection completely, put Clemmie on, would you, son?"

Joel gratefully handed the earpiece her way, needing a moment alone. "He wants to talk to you."

Once she took the phone, he moved back to the sofa and took a seat. He pulled his handkerchief from his suit pocket and wiped his damp lashes. Incredible. After all he'd done, after the lousy way he'd treated those at the refuge, they still held their arms out to him and called him family.

He realized then how much he had missed that. . .missed them.

He wondered if part of the reason Clemmie was able to get through to him had to do with the familiarity he'd felt toward her before knowing she was Clemmie. Had he sensed the feeling of home in her presence? His "box of a home" didn't feel the same without her there, and he knew if it weren't for his pixie angel he would be in the same dark rut. He still had areas in which he wasn't ready to move forward, still felt issues in resuming his former connection to God and issues all his own that stemmed from guilt. But he had come far in the past week alone, and Clemmie was responsible for the majority of his changed attitude.

Once she ended the call and came back to sit beside him, he spoke.

"I'd like to ask a favor of you."

"Of course, Joel. Anything. You know that." She sounded like her father, and again he felt overwhelmed by the Lyonses' generosity. As a boy he'd never appreciated it, but as a man he could see the many sacrifices her father had made and the good heart that led him to those decisions.

"Without you I wouldn't be doing this, Clemmie. It's a lot to ask, but I'd like you to go with me to the doc and"—he shrugged—"just be around through whatever happens."

"I wouldn't dream of leaving your side at a time like this."

Her fervent admission encouraged him, but he shook his head. "There's no telling how long this'll take. I know your stay here is nearing an end. You mentioned you were only staying through the summer, and summer's almost over."

"I. . .um. . ." She sounded nervous with the way she hedged. "Fact is, I already asked and received my parents' permission to stay as long as you need me here, in case it came to that. I was, um, hoping you might ask."

He smiled at her shy admission and again reached for her hand. "Clemmie, you're a true gem. I don't know what I'd do without you."

"I'll always be here for you, Joel."

❧

Clemmie rushed for the exit door, feeling as if a clamp squeezed her lungs; she couldn't breathe. Her excuse for needed air had been flimsy; she was sure Joel had seen through her guise and knew so when she heard the hospital door open and the taps of his cane.

With unbelievable precision, he found her where she leaned against the brick wall of the building and put his hand to her arm. "I'm sorry. I should have told you."

She wasn't sure if she was angrier with him for keeping such a dangerous fact hidden or for refusing to get help when he knew it was crucial.

She whipped around to face him. "I can't believe you, Joel. The doctor said you could have lost your life, that every day death is a possibility if something goes wrong. That whatever is causing this awful pressure to your cranium and optic nerve could push a little the wrong way and do severe damage— likely kill you. And you knew. All this time, *you knew*? Why didn't you go through the surgery before now? Why?"

She felt frustrated with both him and the doctor, who'd so matter-of-factly stated that the medical profession still remained in the dark when it came to head traumas such as Joel had suffered. At the same time, he confirmed to Joel that his erratic mood swings and severe headaches were likely related to his condition but that the operation itself was extremely risky. He could die either way. It had been the first time she realized Joel still suffered any type of headache, though he'd told the doctor he hadn't had one in over a month.

"I told you." Joel's voice was grim and quiet. "That's all I wanted at the time. To die."

Hearing him speak the words she'd just thought, Clemmie shuddered. She simply couldn't believe it. Oh, she'd heard him say it before, but she'd never believed he would go to such extremes, to neglect the value of life and refuse the surgery. She had been under the mistaken impression that the operation was a recommendation to regain his sight, not a necessity to prevent probable death. Based on what the doctor had said during the lengthy consultation, Joel was extremely lucky to be alive.

"Hey. . ." He slid his hand down her arm and found her hand, squeezing it. "If this is too much for you and you want to pull out, I'll understand."

She blinked in disbelief, staring into his eyes, which were soft with remorse. Here he'd been told that his life was at risk with every day, every minute that passed, and *he* felt bad for *her*? Of course, he'd had over a year to deal with the doctor's grim prognosis.

"Just try and get rid of me, Joel Litton. I'm no quitter. And neither are you. I'll be beside you every step of the way."

His answering smile helped to soothe the ache in her heart.

"No, Clemmie, that's one good thing that can be said about us. For all our stubborn natures, neither of us is willing to give in and concede defeat."

In the days that followed, she reminded herself of his words often.

Now understanding the severity of his condition, she didn't urge him to take part in social activities as before, but she wouldn't allow him to stay confined in his box, either. In between tests and more tests she found a peaceful spot near the lake and encouraged Joe to go there with her. Soon it became a ritual. There, they picnicked and relaxed and laughed and talked about the old days and the present ones. At the lake, they never discussed the upcoming surgery or anything related to his condition, neither of them wanting to create a damper on the peace they'd both found and shared.

Over the next two weeks Joel suffered two of his bad headaches when Clemmie came to do her usual cleaning. Her heart clenched with fear at the terrible pain he suffered. She did her best to help, putting cold compresses on his forehead, massaging his temples, and making him hot, soothing beverages that helped when her own head ached. To her chagrin, very little she did took any pain away, but he thanked her and held onto her hand like a lifeline. Often she stayed until he managed to sleep and even past then, sitting beside his bed or quietly straightening his home.

In her heart, she felt like his wife, and all she did was with the great love she felt for Joel, which only deepened as time passed. She hoped one day he might feel the same strong affection for her, though she doubted it. He hadn't kissed her once since he discovered her identity, though he did accept her hugs and often held her hand. But she resigned herself to the idea that he'd gone back to thinking of her as a kid sister....

And Sheridan Wallace clearly wanted him back.

The woman had visited Joel four times since the picnic— that Clemmie knew of, because she'd been there when it happened. She wished she could loathe the elegant blond. But irony of ironies, she found herself liking Sheridan, even coming to regard her as a friend. That Sheridan and Joel got along well didn't escape Clemmie's notice, and she resolved to bury her dream once more, if she must, in order to help Joel realize his. And if that meant having Sheridan by his side, Clemmie would learn to accept his choice and only be to him what she'd always been—a friend.

No matter her firm resolution, the idea of Joel belonging to any other woman made her heart feel as if it were breaking. Somehow, she would get through the long weeks.

Somehow, she must.

seventeen

"Hey, ole pal. What are you doing all alone? I would have thought Clemmie would be here the day before you go under the knife." Herbert greeted Joel as he approached his porch. "As a matter of fact, with the way you two have been, I'm surprised not to find her glued to your side."

Joel took Herbert's ribbing in stride. He didn't want anyone to know he was worried he wouldn't survive. That fear was uppermost in his mind.

"She went with Hannah to the train station."

"Oh, right! Her parents are coming in today, and Darcy, too, from what I hear. It'll be swell to see them again."

"Yeah. Swell."

"I see Clemmie made one of your favorite desserts again. What's eating you? No appetite?"

Joel recalled the barely touched peach pie he'd set on the porch. "Not much. Want the rest?"

"Don't mind if I do."

Joel handed Herbert the plate, and Herbert chuckled.

"Remember the days when we would fight over who would get one of Darcy's pies for her contests? Mmm. Clemmie ·makes them just as good. You'd be a fool to let a doll like that go," Herbert observed with his mouth full. "And you can't tell me you just care about her like a little sister either. I've seen the way you are with her."

"I'm hardly in any shape to consider a relationship right now. Thea sent you over here to keep me company so I wouldn't brood, didn't she?"

"And then there's Sheridan. What a knockout—and sweet as Christmas candy, to boot. She's made it as obvious as the nose on your face that she's stuck on you, coming here like she does to visit and flagging you down at church every week."

"I can't see my nose, and I told you I'm not interested."

"To pass up either one of them, you must be bloodless or dead."

"No, but come tomorrow, check again."

"Hey now, don't go talking like that." Herbert's effusiveness dissolved into gruff sincerity. "You have a team of people praying—us, Clemmie and her family, Darcy, Brent, all those at the refuge, Sheridan, Paisley, their mom, Hannah, her mom and dad..."

"Okay, okay. I get the picture. Still, you never know what could happen."

"Then it's a good thing you've made things right with your Maker, wouldn't you say?"

Joel couldn't agree more. He couldn't say what led him to reach out to God again—maybe a conglomeration of all that had happened in the past two months. One morning as he sat alone before Clemmie arrived, he felt so empty, so bleak, and he recalled much of the encouragement she'd given and what he had recently heard the pastor say. God's love was eternal. Nothing Joel could do would prevent God from loving him, and he'd seen a shadow of such love in the way Clemmie's father had treated him, had always treated him, no matter how badly Joel had behaved. Perhaps that had been the last blow needed to break the stony barrier that had encased his heart.

"Yes," he told Herbert, "I know the Lord will be with me. And if I wake up and see your ugly mug, then I'll know it wasn't my time to go yet. And if I wake up and see the angels and the face of God... Well, either way I can't lose, can I?"

Herbert clapped him on the shoulder. "That's the spirit! Just don't let Clemmie hear you talk of dying."

"No, I'd never hear the end of it. This has really hit her hard."

"She cares a lot about you."

"I know." Joel grew somber.

"Sheridan, too, for that matter. You were so afraid of stepping foot off the property, afraid to be seen and of what people would think. Now you have two sweet gals eager to wear your ring on their finger. A fella should be so lucky."

"You have no reason to complain. Thea is one great lady to put up with the likes of you. And me."

"Don't I know it? I suppose I should share the news, since it'll be obvious to everyone soon, but we're getting another little Miller this winter."

Joel's smile was genuine. "Well, what do you know? Congratulations, buddy."

"And you need to stick around longer so *all* our children can get to know their uncle Joel. The girls think the world of you, though I can't say why. You really can be incorrigible at times—my word, now I sound like our old schoolmaster!"

Joel snorted a laugh at his friend's nutty impersonation of Brent. Over the past few weeks he'd spent time with Herbert's daughters, telling them stories of his and Herbert's childhood at the refuge. He'd even learned to tolerate their wretched cat, which had developed a habit of making its home on his lap. Absentmindedly, his hand went to the silky soft fur and stroked it, a rumbling purr soon following.

"You know, old buddy, you're really not half bad with children. Maybe you should consider settling down and raising your own family."

Herbert clearly wasn't going to quit. Rather than go into both reasons again: that he couldn't ask a woman to share his life when he was out of work and that he didn't know from day to day if he'd be around long enough to put that ring on her finger, Joel settled for reason A.

"If the operation's a success, I'll need to find a job and a decent place to live. No offense, old pal, but no way am I going to continue living out my days in this shed."

"Good. And you're right. Women like windows. This place hasn't a one. They want plenty of space to decorate for all the knickknacks they bring home, too."

"Will you just get out of here?"

Herbert chuckled. "Seriously, I'll talk to my boss. I'm sure he'll take you back. He likes you. Said it was a shame to lose such a good worker. Said you might even have the makings of becoming a journalist one day."

"Mr. Thomas would disagree. I was one of his worst pupils when it came to writing reports and those awful poems." This wasn't the first time Herbert had told Joel their boss's opinion of his potential, but before, Joel hadn't cared. Now he felt that soft emotion clutch his insides again, making him tear up—something that had been happening a lot of late.

"Herbert!" Thea called from the back porch. "I need you a minute, honey."

Herbert groaned. "Duty calls. I just hope it's not about that silly painting she got at the bazaar. That woman must have made me move it fifty times already, to find the 'perfect spot.' I'm beginning to think one doesn't exist."

Joel smiled. "Thank you again, my friend. For everything. I know we rib each other a lot and don't always get along, but you've been a pal, helping me out like you have. I don't know how I would have made it without you."

"You're not going to start waxing poetic and get all sappy on me?" Herbert's mocking horror teased, but Joel heard the softness clutch his voice, proof he was also getting emotional.

"Aw, go on and get out of here before I take it all back."

"Yup, there's the Joel I know so well. But this isn't good-bye, so don't treat it like one. That said, now I'm going to get sappy—you've always been like a big brother to me. Even if you were a worm at times."

Joel laughed. "Would you just go? And Herbert," he added once he heard his friend's steps move off the porch and to the grass. "Feeling's mutual. On both counts."

Herbert's laughter as he departed made Joel smile again.

No matter what happened on the operating table, God had blessed him with a caring family at the refuge, parents who were his not by blood but by heart, and good friends. Not everyone could claim so much to be thankful for.

At least he'd had that.

❧

"Clemmie, luv, stop yer pacing before you wear a trail in the floor."

She turned toward Darcy who sat on one of several benches against the wall in the stark, white hospital corridor where relatives waited while loved ones were in the operating room. "It's been hours. Why haven't we heard anything by now?"

Her mother came up behind and hugged her. "The doctor said surgery such as his could last quite a long time, dear. There's nothing unusual about that." Clemmie felt grateful for her family's support, sure she would have fallen apart if they weren't there. She settled her head back against her mother's shoulder, holding on to the arms she'd looped around her waist. "You need to curb that impatient streak of yours and settle down, sweetheart."

"I know I should, but I just can't, Mama. This is Joel we're talking about."

"I know. And you love him, don't you? Not like a brother but as something much more."

"I've always loved him," Clemmie admitted. "But it's different than when I was a child. It's grown deeper now that I'm a woman. Matured and changed. And no, not like a brother at all." She flushed, remembering his passionate kisses.

"And how does he feel about you?"

"That's the question of the century," she replied dismally. "I wish I knew. At times I think he still regards me like a little sis and good friend. At other times I think he wishes we had more—or maybe that's my own wishful thinking?" She sighed. "I should just be grateful he didn't boot me out the door when I let him believe I was someone else and he found out I wasn't." Her words, upon hearing them, made little sense, but she felt emotionally drained and didn't bother to clarify. Nor had she slept much the night before, anxious for Joel.

"That. . .was a mistake," her mother gently admonished. "But I understand you didn't mean harm. I've done a good many things I wish I hadn't. A good many. But God always intervened when I asked Him to mend things, just like He did for you. I still wish to this day I'd never met Eric. . .yet if I never had, he might not be where he is, with his own loving family, of all things, and working in his soup kitchen mission. God certainly has a peculiar way of working things out."

Clemmie turned to look at her mother and noticed new lines of strain etched around her mouth and between her brows. Yet with her glowing skin, dark auburn hair, and pale green eyes, she had an unearthly beauty not many women did. "Have you talked to him recently?" She still found it odd that her mother and the villain who'd made her life a living purgatory, even trying to kill her more than once, had actually made amends.

"Just the yearly Christmas cards, as you know, compliments of his wife, I would imagine. Nothing more. I understand he and Bill Thomas still correspond by letter and the telephone. They were gangsters together in the old life, working for that awful Piccoli man. Oh, it just seems so strange talking about those horrid days in such a calm fashion. Time truly heals all wounds, and God does work miracles. He can for Joel, too."

"I know, Mama. Still, it's so hard."

"What you need is an amusing tale to take your mind off things." Darcy patted the empty chair next to her. "Come sit beside me, luv, and let me tell you what mischief that new boy Quentin has been up to now."

"Darcy," her mother warned with a slight laugh mixed with a groan. "It's not nice to tell tales."

"And you don't think she'll be gettin' an earful on her return? He didn't exactly do his misdeeds in private, Charleigh. Maybe she can give us an idea of how to get through to him." Darcy smiled at Clemmie while continuing to talk to her mother. "She always did have such a good head on her shoulders."

Except when it came to her own choices. Still, it did help

hearing about the wild antics of the new young reformer, what the refuge's problem children called themselves. In between spurts of quiet laughter over the food fight he'd caused and shocked horror that he'd almost burned down the woodshed after experimenting with a cigar he'd snatched from Grandfather's box, with his own gang of boys who looked up to him, Clemmie realized how much like Joel the new boy was.

Soon her father, Hannah, and Hannah's parents returned with sandwiches; and Clemmie felt relieved and surprised that the nurses didn't throw them out, their number had become so large. They kept their voices to a dull murmur, respecting where they were, Clemmie's heart clenched in gratitude when her father gathered them all around to pray for Joel. She knew her father could see past her false smiles and wavering courage. He had always been able to read her well.

Hannah sat close and held her hand, offering reassurances while the hands of the clock slowly made their revolutions.

Once.

Twice.

Again.

At last a nurse came forward, and Clemmie jumped to her feet. "Joel Litton—how. . .how is he?"

"Your friend made it through surgery."

Clemmie felt as if she might fall and held strongly to Hannah's arm. "Can I see him?"

"Not until tomorrow. He's under anesthesia and will be for some time."

She didn't add what Clemmie feared most—*if he wakes up.*

"Please. I just want a peek. I won't go inside."

"He won't know you're there."

"I don't care. Please. . ."

"It's against hospital policy. . . ." The nurse's eyes gentled as if she could sense Clemmie's urgency to see for herself. "All right. Just a quick peek through the door."

"Thank you."

She followed the nurse down a series of corridors before they stopped at a room. The nurse smiled and inclined her head, opening the door.

The area was dark, but Clemmie could see his form on the bed. The top of his head and his eyes were swathed in white bandages. From the steady rise and fall of his chest, she knew what the nurse told her must be true.

Joel was alive; he had survived the dangerous operation.

"Thank You, God," she whispered and, not caring what the nurse might think, blew Joel a soft, trembling kiss before turning to rejoin her family.

eighteen

Joel awoke to familiar dark. And pain. Excruciating pain, more severe than any headache; he groaned in agony. It took awhile to remember where he was and why. The voices of those in his room—nurses? doctors?—soon became blurred, and he began to feel woozy.

He woke off and on, with no idea how much time passed—minutes? Hours? Days? It was too much trouble to figure out. In his more lucid moments, he listened to the murmuring voices, his sole connection to reality, and tried to figure out their identity. Soon a soft, husky one grew familiar to him, and he reached out.

"Clemmie?" he rasped.

Instantly, her soft, warm hand wrapped around his, and he relaxed.

"I'm here, Joel. Is the pain very bad?"

"Awful."

"Perhaps you need more morphine. Nurse?"

"Wait, no. . .before they dope me up again. . .and I forget everything. . .thank you."

"You don't have to keep thanking me. I want to be here."

"How long. . ."

"Five days since the surgery. They. . .they weren't sure you'd wake up."

He heard the tightness of tears clutch her voice as she fought them back.

"I'm here."

"Thank God."

He heard the nurse approach and felt Clemmie begin to move away. He tightened his hold on her hand. "Don't go."

Her other hand covered his. "I won't."

His lucidity gave way to the drug pulling him back into the dark of oblivion.

So his life progressed. He awoke at times more aware, at other times feeling as if he were in a strange dream that made no sense. Sometimes the pain was unbearable. Others, it was more manageable, and on those days, Clemmie read to him from her book, a little at a time. He couldn't always follow the story, but just the sound of her low, gentle voice soothed him. By the time she reached the end of the novel, he was able to understand and felt satisfied that Christian had met his goal and found God.

Sheridan also came to visit, as kind and concerned as Clemmie, and she often kissed his cheek in parting, telling him he must rest and get better. She would make some man a fine wife one day, he thought after one of her visits.

At times the drug tricked his mind and he felt confused. He was sure he'd called Sheridan Clemmie more than once and had done the same to Clemmie. He just hoped both women understood if he did and weren't hurt by his lack of clear thinking.

❧

Clemmie felt breathless after her run up the stairs. How, oh how could she have overslept? It was past noon!

She hurried along the corridor to Joel's room, stopping short at the sight of Sheridan sitting close to him, on the edge of his bed.

"You know I'm always here for you, Joel," Clemmie heard her say.

"Don't leave. . .I was a fool, not to know. . .not to admit how I feel. . . ."

"Shhh. It's all right. You rest now. I'm not going anywhere."

"I want you with me. . .always. . .a lifetime."

Clemmie watched in stricken horror as Sheridan took his hand in hers and bent to touch her lips to his, keeping them fixed there.

Standing in utter shock, Clemmie felt as if she'd been

socked in the gut, worse than any injury from the fights she'd been in as a little tomboy. Quickly, lest Sheridan notice her, she backed away from the door and retraced her way to the entrance, her steps growing faster until she was almost at a run. Tears blinded her as she rushed from the building and hurried to cross the street. A piercing squeal of brakes made her stop in horror when she realized an oncoming car came only a few feet from hitting her.

Shakily, she stepped back to the curb. Once the glowering driver passed, she made her way across, careful this time, her heart so heavy she wasn't sure how she could walk with the weight of her understanding. Joel had clearly made his choice. She had known this could happen the moment she laid eyes on Sheridan and realized they'd once been more than friends, and she must come to terms with his decision.

But the sight of their kiss brought such fiery pain to her chest she didn't see how she'd be able to visit again, not with Sheridan there. And from the loving and personal revelations she'd heard, Joel's choice of a girlfriend never planned on leaving his side.

Clemmie had promised him she would be with him through the entire ordeal, and she had. But clearly he didn't need her anymore.

☙

"I can't believe you're going home in less than a week!" Hannah complained. "It seems like yesterday when you got here."

Clemmie finished looking through the box of movie star photos that were Hannah's treasure. Their perfect faces and slim bodies made her feel inferior, but she was what she was. It cheered her only a little to learn that Myrna, Claudette, and Greer were all redheads, too. She visited the movie theater only on rare occasions and had never seen their movies, though she'd heard about them, of course.

"Have you talked to Joel since he was discharged from the hospital?"

Clemmie gave her friend a sharp look. Hannah knew she hadn't.

"I hear they took the bandages off. Sheridan told me when I ran into her the other day. I figured you must know and just forgot to mention it?"

The query sounded strange, even to Clemmie's ears, since most of her days had been filled with Joel and keeping Hannah informed of almost every detail. Forgetting to mention such a huge milestone would be absurd.

"Yes, I know. I rang the hospital and learned the news from that nice nurse who let me see him after his surgery." She tried to look busy as she gathered the glossies and tapped them on her lap to straighten them. "He can see again. Isn't it wonderful?"

Hannah's hand rested over hers, stopping her agitated movements. Carefully she slipped the pictures from Clemmie's hands. "And you didn't think to tell me this amazing news?"

"I've had a lot on my mind, what with packing and such. I assumed you would hear from your mother. She mentioned she's gone to visit him. Your father, too."

Hannah shook her head at Clemmie's weak answer. "But you haven't gone to see him again, have you? Not since that day you came home from the hospital looking for all the world as if your best friend had just died."

"No. I haven't."

"Why?" Hannah insisted. "Did you two have a quarrel?"

"Nothing like that. Life doesn't always make sense, Hannah. That's something you'll learn one day." Seeing that her friend wouldn't give up, Clemmie sought a more complete explanation. "I just felt it was time he took charge of his life without my help, now that he's past the surgery."

"So you've said before—and it still doesn't make one bit of sense! He was everything to you, and now you're pushing him aside?"

Clemmie shrugged.

Hannah exhaled loudly. "I'm not a child, Clemmie. I know life doesn't always play fair, though I haven't had much to complain about. But, well, you are going to tell him good-bye before you go home, aren't you?"

"I don't know. Maybe."

"Maybe?" Hannah threw the pictures back into the box, a sign of just how frustrated she was. "If it weren't for you, he would never have had that surgery in the first place. He'd still be living alone in his box."

"He still is. Though he's been trying to find a place." She clamped her lips shut, realizing her slip.

"So you *have* been keeping tabs on him!"

"Of course. I can't just forget him. I still talk to Thea on occasion."

"Then why. . . ?"

Clemmie rose from Hannah's bed, where they'd been poring over photos for the umpteenth time since her arrival in Connecticut. "I don't want to talk about this right now—please. I think I'll take a walk by the pond. I need some fresh air."

"I'll come with you." Hannah was already putting the lid on her box and sliding off the bed.

"No, please. I—I just need time alone to think." She smiled. "Don't worry. I'll be back in time for supper."

Hannah nodded, clearly concerned, but Clemmie couldn't talk about Joel. She knew her friend was right: She couldn't leave without telling him good-bye. But she dreaded finding Sheridan there and didn't think she could handle seeing them together. No, she had to do it. She simply must stop behaving like a wounded pup licking her wounds and face him again. She wasn't a child; it was time to stop behaving like one. Yes, she hurt. But she had to learn to face her pain head-on and not hide from it. Isn't that what she'd told Joel for weeks?

The air was brisk, invigorating from the coming autumn. She took deep breaths as she strolled along the beautiful grounds to the gardens and beyond, to the tranquil pond sheltered among towering trees whose foliage had begun to blaze with color. Strangely, though the area didn't look the same, it reminded her of her spot at the lake with Joel and the ease they'd shared with one another there.

She felt grateful God had used her, even her mistake, to help Joel, and that their friendship had strengthened beyond what it ever was. But she couldn't help the tears that trickled past her lashes as she wished for something that would never be.

How long she stood there, she didn't know, but she had the oddest sensation of being watched. A prickle danced along her neck down to her spine. She wiped her eyes with her sleeve then looked over her shoulder.

And froze.

Joel stood not ten feet away.

❧

Weeks after his surgery Joel wondered and worried when Clemmie never showed up to visit again. He asked Herbert and Thea, but they had no idea why she stayed away. He had phoned Hannah's, but the butler always stated that Miss Lyons wasn't home. It wasn't like Clemmie to disappear from his life when she had forced her way into it more than three months before. He was sure she would be there when the doctor removed the bandages and share with him either the pain of failure or the triumph of sight. The doctor had waited as long as he could until he told Joel he had other patients and could wait no longer. Joel reluctantly agreed. Sheridan had come, and he'd been grateful for her company, but he'd wanted Clemmie there since she'd been a huge support to him and the reason he'd made the leap to pursue the operation.

Upon opening his eyes once the doctor removed the final bandage, Joel had at first been blinded by the doctor's flashlight, though the room had been darkened. After more than a year of empty black and dark gray, colors had come back to his world—colors and shapes—a world he remembered and now appreciated all the more for having lost it.

But nothing prepared him for his first sight of Clemmie as a woman.

The sun's rays slanted through the trees and reflected off

her hair—a lively mix of light reds and golds that almost touched her shoulders in a wavy fashion of the day. Her eyes were the most fascinating shade of dusky green with the sun bringing out yellow flecks, obvious even at this distance, her brows gently sloping in light brown arcs. Her face appeared as smooth and fair as porcelain. Her lips were wide, full, perfect, and her cheeks rosy—whether natural or from her walk or embarrassment at finding him there, he couldn't guess. Full-figured like her mother—not slender, not plump—she wore a simple brown skirt and creamy white blouse that outlined every curve of her, and she used none of the cosmetics that so many women seemed to feel necessary.

Joel stood thunderstruck. She wasn't plain, as she'd led him to believe. Nor did she have Sheridan's fair, classic beauty. Clemmie was so much more than common or a carbon copy of others who tried to emulate the movie starlets of the day. In her simplicity and with her unique coloring, she was magnificent!

As long as he lived, he knew he would never forget this moment. . . .

"Joel?" She licked her lower lip nervously. "I—I didn't expect you. Is something the matter?"

His eyes on her mouth, he answered her. "I could ask you the same thing." He lifted his gaze to hers. "Why did you stop visiting me?"

She pressed a pale hand to her heart. "I–I'm sorry. And I'm so glad you got your sight back."

"Are you?"

"Of course! You really need to ask such a silly question?"

He moved closer and noticed a light sprinkling of adorable freckles dotting her nose and cheeks. "Why weren't you there?"

"What?"

He noticed how her chest rose and fell sharply, could see the pulse that beat in the hollow of her creamy throat and the manner in which her natural, pale rose–colored lips parted in uncertainty. He could feast his eyes upon the vision of her all day.

"You heard me. Why weren't you there when the bandages came off?"

"Oh." She lifted her chin a little as if bolstering herself. "I knew Sheridan would be there for you."

He closed the remaining distance between them. "I wanted you."

She inhaled a shaky breath, her incredible eyes flickering wider. "I–I'm sorry." She took a sudden step back, clearly flustered. "How's your girlfriend these days?"

He drew his brows together at her odd choice of words. "My girlfriend?"

"Sheridan," she clarified as if he should know it.

"Sheridan's not my girlfriend."

"Of course she is! I saw her kiss you—"

He watched as the flush on her face spread, extending down the slim column of her neck, and her green-gold eyes flared wider. This close, he could see the curly spikes of each fringe of her soft brown lashes. Wet lashes. She'd been crying.

"Sheridan's not my girlfriend," he repeated. "And I don't want her to be."

"But I heard you!"

"Heard me?"

Her skin took on a deeper shade of rose, and she bit the lip she had moistened again. "At the hospital. Y–you asked her never to leave you. Told her that you'd been wrong about not admitting something and. . .and that you wanted her with you forever. I heard you. . . ." Her voice trailed off weakly as he opened his eyes wider in understanding.

"Clemmie, I thought Sheridan was you."

"What? That's impossible. We sound nothing alike."

"The drugs they gave me confused me, making voices hard to understand. Remember how sometimes I called you Sheridan? I did the same with her and called her Clemmie."

"I. . ."

She stood, her mouth open wide, her eyes dazed.

He moved forward, closing the distance between them, and took her hands in his. "I wasn't going to speak up, not until I had a chance to talk with your father, not until you turned eighteen, not until I understood the distance you'd put between us. Now that I know, I can't wait any longer. There's no girlfriend, Clemmie. Do you understand?"

Dully, she nodded.

"But there is this girl who nagged me and tormented me and wouldn't let me concede to failure. Who helped me face my fears and put my past behind me so I could dream again. And it's this girl, this amazing woman, I want to call my wife. I held back saying anything because my life was so uncertain, especially with the prospect of death hanging over my head. But now there's no reason to hold back."

Motionless, she stared as if turned to a porcelain doll. She didn't even blink.

"Clemmie. . .do you understand what I'm saying?" He dropped to one knee and felt her hands tremble in his. "I love you. Only you. I have for some time, but I was too stubborn to admit it. Now I do." His eyes searched her face for some sign, some encouragement, and he blindly struck forward. "Clementine Lyons, will you do me the honor of becoming my wife? I don't want to live another day in this world without you."

She blinked, hard and repeatedly, her breaths coming fast. All the rose color that had suffused her face drained away, leaving it almost stark white. Worried about her reaction and thinking he would need to catch her if she should suddenly collapse, he jumped to his feet. "Is this too soon—"

"You want to marry me? *Me*? . . .You love me?" she whispered in disbelief, such a look of utter astonishment crossing her features that Joel couldn't help himself. He cradled her face in his hands and kissed her, taking pleasure in tasting her lips after so long denying himself the satisfaction and learning their soft, warm texture again. When he pulled away, they were both breathless.

"Are you convinced yet?"

She gave a sobbing little laugh. He felt entranced by her smile, which lit up her face. Her eyes, already beautiful, shone with happiness, like jewels. "I'm not sure." Her voice came a little stronger, an intriguing mix of teasing and shyness. "It takes awhile to get facts straight in my head sometimes. I might need more convincing?"

With a low chuckle at her hopeful suggestion, Joel gladly accepted the challenge.

nineteen

"Pinch me."

With a mischievous grin, Hannah obeyed.

"Ow." Clemmie laughed. "Not so hard. You don't want to bruise me, do you?"

"You wanted to make certain you're awake, right?"

Clemmie smiled. She hadn't been able to stop smiling all morning. "Oh, Hannah, is it true? Am I getting the dream I always wished for?"

"To have me for your maid of honor?" Hannah teased. "Or to wear such a pretty dress and have so many people fawning over you?"

Darcy, who'd just finished pinning up Clemmie's hair, snorted out a laugh.

"To marry Joel, silly," Clemmie replied, rolling her eyes heavenward.

"Oh, then yes, I'd have to say you're getting your dream. And you do look gorgeous in that dress."

"Don't I look go-geous in my dress?" Clemmie's eight-year-old sister, Belle, demanded, twirling so the satin folds billowed out.

"You'd look a mite prettier if you didn't still have traces of that black eye," her mother reproved.

"Can't help it, Mama. Quentin started it. He's so dumb."

"Reminds you of Clint and Miranda, doesn't it?" Clemmie's mother asked Darcy. "Those two were at each other's throats night and day as children. Now they're married with two children of their own!"

"Eww!" Belle wrinkled her nose. "I'm never gonna marry, not in a million jillion years. And I'd never marry him!"

"Oh dear. That sounds like what Miranda used to say

about Clint when she was your age."

"Better take good care of that wedding dress of your mother's, Clemmie," Darcy teased. "Your sister might be needing it soon."

"Perish the thought," Clemmie's mother said with a laugh. "I'm losing one daughter today. Don't go and marry off my baby years before her time."

"You're not losing me, Mama. We'll visit every holiday. More, if Joel's job at the paper allows it."

"Or you could both move back to the refuge," her mother said hopefully. "Plenty of room there. And I'm sure we can find something for Joel to do."

Across the room, Angel laughed, and Clemmie turned her attention to another of her oldest and dearest friends.

"Better elope with Joel while you can," Angel teased. "Before your mother takes it into her head to pack you both up in her trunk and take you back home to live."

"Now there's an idea," Darcy teased as if she were serious.

Clemmie smiled at their banter, thankful for her family and friends, even if they were a bit absurd at times. In her pale lilac bridesmaid's dress, Angel looked splendid. They all did. Thea, advanced with child, hadn't been able to be a bridesmaid, but Angel, who was only four months into her second pregnancy and bloomed like a flower, had yet to show. Clemmie had defied convention to have her married friend in her wedding party, thrilled to be with her again. Roland and Angel had come from their home, thirty minutes away by train, while Angel's mother, Lila, never fond of crowds after the horrors of living in a circus freak show, stayed home with little Everett.

Many from the refuge had arrived at the home of Hannah's uncle. Although he hadn't expected them, old boyhood chums of Joel's, now married and moved on, made an appearance: Tommy, Lance, and the childhood rivals Clint and Miranda. Not only were Clint and Miranda parents, but Miranda had also achieved her dream of becoming a teacher.

Clemmie's heart felt near to bursting with joy. She'd heard other women sometimes suffered from pre-wedding jitters. But Clemmie had known what she wanted since she was a young girl: Joel. The only emotion she felt besides delirium was eagerness to begin the ceremony that would transform her dream into reality.

"You look lovely." Her mother moved forward, attaching her filmy veil and adjusting it. With teary eyes, she examined every inch of Clemmie's appearance, smiling with approval. "I'm so happy for you, dear. Joel may have been a rapscallion as a lad, but he's turned into a fine man."

"The best, Mama."

"Are you ready? We should be leaving for the church."

"I think I've been ready for Joel all my life."

Her mother laughed. "Well then, let's go and make you his bride."

§

"Nervous, old man?" Herbert stood beside Joel, checking his image in the mirror.

Joel wrenched the confounded drooping tie from his neck. Normal ties were bad enough. With a bow tie he might as well be all thumbs. "I'm managing."

"I can tell. You're shaking so bad it's a wonder I don't hear your knees knocking together."

"You're supposed to be my best man," Joel groused. "Not my worst."

"Mind if I barge in?"

"Mr. Lyons." Joel's nervousness peaked. "Sir. . ."

"Now, Joel, none of that. I told you, you're to call me Dad." Stewart Lyons walked into the room, as impressive as ever, his height and build rivaling any young man's. His hair had turned almost all silver, and Joel reckoned he was responsible for a number of them. "Having trouble, I see. I always did hate those things. Mind if I take a go at it?"

Joel shook his head. "No, sir. Dad." He swallowed hard.

"Sir Dad—now that would make for an interesting byline,"

Herbert observed in amusement. "Picture it: Sir Dad gives Fair Daughter away to Black Knight."

"One more crack and I'm booting you out the door," Joel darkly replied.

Mr. Lyons chuckled as he took the ends of the offending tie and expertly twisted and turned the material until he'd achieved a perfect bow. "You boys still have trouble getting along?"

"Not all the time, sir—Dad."

Herbert snorted.

Joel didn't mind Herbert's ribbing as much as he pretended. It took his mind off the upcoming minutes, which were advancing like a herd of wild cattle. He loved Clemmie, didn't doubt that. And he wanted her as his wife. It was this ceremony, which had grown from the intended private nuptials to a gigantic circus, courtesy of Clemmie's wealthy grandfather and Hannah's just as wealthy uncle, who'd offered his full staff and banquet hall for the reception. Clemmie had been in her element during the past two months of planning, thrilled with the prospect of the whole elaborate shindig, so for his bride, Joel would bear it. Strange that he used to always enjoy being the center of attention and now wanted to run from it. He assumed more than a year of being a hermit had caused the change.

"Herbert," Clemmie's father said, "can you give us a moment?"

"Sure." Herbert looked back and forth between them before leaving the small room where the pastor's aide had led them to wait.

Joel swallowed nervously, the awkward bow tie pushing against his Adam's apple.

"I know we talked last night in depth, but there are a few things I want to say before you go out there."

Uh-oh. Here it comes. The warning never to treat Clemmie badly, not that he would, but the threat of what might happen if he should.

Joel gave a tense nod, preparing himself.

"I'm proud of you, son. Proud of who you are today. Your life has been riddled with bad choices and mistakes, and it takes a real man of strong character to learn from those bad decisions and strive to better himself. Sometimes adversity brings great strength—and you've shown that. Even your boss at the paper raves about what a remarkable employee you are. I only wish Brent could hear for himself what an upstanding man his wayward pupil became, but of course someone had to stay behind with the children."

Joel blinked furiously, fighting back the tears that stung his eyes. "Sir. . .Dad. If it weren't for your patience and generosity and this past summer with your daughter, I would have never tried."

"My daughter, soon to be your wife, eh?" He smiled. "I never would have believed this day would come all those years ago, but having seen you together, you two do make a fine couple. I can see how much you love my baby girl, and I know you'll treat her well."

"Yes. . .Dad. Clemmie means everything to me. I only want to make her happy."

Her father clapped a hand to Joel's back. "Well then, what do you say we go and take the first step in making that possible?"

With Herbert behind him, Joel followed Mr. Lyons to the front of the church, his eyes widening at the number of people who filled the pews. *Good gravy!* He didn't remember them inviting this many—but word must have spread. Spotting old faces from his past with a shock, he had a feeling he knew who'd been the culprit. He glanced his best man's way with narrowed eyes.

"You told everyone who knows me, didn't you?" Joel whispered to Herbert as Clemmie's father took a side aisle to the back of the church.

"So, what's the problem? Now that you can see and are about to marry the gal who probably loves you most in this world, there's no longer any reason for the big secret. It's about time people knew you're back among the living, and today is a major cause for celebration. Wouldn't you say?"

"Hmm. Maybe I chose my best man right after all."

"Who else were you going to ask, the cat?"

Joel softly chuckled. "No. The job would only do for my best brother."

The organ music started, and they turned to face the back. Joel watched the short procession of bridesmaids accompanied by Clemmie's brother and two friends at the paper who Joel had asked to be his groomsmen. Then Clemmie appeared in a satin ivory gown, and Joel forgot all else.

She looked stunning. Amazing.

And she was his. Minutes away from becoming his wife.

Why had God blessed him so profoundly?

Because He loves you, Joel.

Clemmie's answer to him during his weeks of soul-searching rose in his mind at the moment her gaze found and held his.

To deserve such love, as God's, as Clemmie's. . .he couldn't begin to understand it, but he would do all he could to honor them both the rest of his life.

As the pastor asked who gave this woman to be his wife, and her father answered "I do," taking her hand and putting it in Joel's, he wondered if there was such a thing as heaven on earth because he felt he must be living in it.

❧

Clemmie floated on clouds. Throughout the ceremony, she never took her gaze from Joel's, and he only glanced away when accepting the ring from Herbert.

"I take you, Clementine Marielle Lyons, as my lawfully wedded wife. . . ." The vows he quietly spoke were sweet music to her ears.

"I take you, Joel Timothy Litton, as my lawfully wedded husband. . . ." She made her promise to him softly, the expression of all that was in her heart, and saw the shine of tears in his eyes that must reflect her own.

"I now pronounce you man and wife," the pastor said moments later. Joel drew Clemmie close and kissed her before the pastor could finish saying, "You may now kiss your bride," earning low chuckles from some guests and making Clemmie and Joel smile.

Caught up in the resulting flurry, the ceremony complete, they were whisked away to the estate of Hannah's uncle, where an elaborate feast awaited on covered tables.

The affair was extravagant, with friends, family, and neighbors from present and past converging to wish the happy couple well. Clemmie found herself in constant demand, and to her frustration, she barely saw her new husband, who'd been detained by others eager to see him, glad to know he was alive. Suddenly Clemmie came face-to-face with Sheridan. They had sent her an invitation, but Clemmie hadn't believed the woman would attend.

"I wish you all the best." Sheridan's eyes were sincere. "You and Joel both."

Clemmie didn't know what to say and felt bad that if the situation were reversed, she probably wouldn't have shown such graciousness. "I'm glad you came, Sheridan. Really."

"Thank you. I hope we can be friends."

"Of course." Clemmie still felt at a loss.

"Clemmie, it's okay." Sheridan patted her arm. "Everything happened the way it was meant to. Joel loves you very much. He told me so, and I'm just happy to see you both happy."

In that moment, Clemmie became Sheridan's fan, too. "Thank you." She hugged her. "And you're always welcome at our home."

"Clemmie, sweetheart. . ." Joel came up behind her and slipped his arm around her waist. "Everything okay here?"

"Wonderful." She turned a beaming smile on him. "I was just telling Sheridan she must come and pay us a visit—when we find a home, of course."

Joel raised his brow as if surprised, and then he smiled at Sheridan. "I second that invitation."

Sheridan laughed. "Then I accept you both. But right now I think you're being paged."

Clemmie and Joel turned to look behind them. Clint, Miranda, Tommy, and Lance eagerly waved to them.

"Uh-oh," Joel said. "I don't like the looks of this."

The fellows moved into a straight line in the middle of the ballroom floor, facing them, linking arm in arm. Joel's face turned red. "Now I know I don't like it."

Clemmie knew what was coming and bit her lip in an effort not to laugh. After all the mischievous serenading Joel had led his gang in when they were boys, it seemed proper that he should get a taste of his own.

Tommy pulled his harmonica from his pocket and blew a few notes, gaining everyone's attention. Joel groaned and closed his eyes.

The men all hummed off-key notes, getting in tune, then belted out their tribute to the happy couple: "Oh my darlin', oh my darlin', Oh, my daaarlin' Clementine. . . ."

The red flush in Joel's face rushed to his ears. Clemmie giggled.

"You were lost and gone forever, oh my daaarlin' Clementine. . . ."

"Kill me now," he joked under his breath. "Did we really sound that bad?"

"They're just hamming it up. You should be used to it."

"Hmm."

Somehow he lived through the rest of the song, the words changed to reflect what an idiot Joel had been to almost lose her and what a saint she was to take him back.

"Nice to know how they really feel," he said, but she could tell he was amused.

Afterward, amid a lot of backslapping and jibes, Tommy made a toast to the happy couple and expressed his delight that the original "Gang of Reformers" was reunited. "May it be the first of many occasions!" he added. His new wife, Angel's cousin Faye, smiled and winked at him, earning her a huge smile; it was good to see Tommy so happy.

Joel clapped his hands to Tommy's and Lance's shoulders. "Okay, I gotta admit—it's great to see all you lugheads again."

Amid much laughing and jesting, the old gang hugged as a group then split up to gather around one of the tables and talk of old days and new. Clemmie, who'd seen some of their antics and heard about the rest, greatly enjoyed all of it. Miranda excused herself to take care of her and Clint's youngest boy, and the men were in heated discussion over who was the culprit behind an old prank on the schoolmaster. Everyone had a theory. Joel turned to whisper in Clemmie's ear.

"Let's get out of here."

"You mean just leave?"

"I've had enough commotion for one day. But if you want to stay for them showering us in rice and all that. . ."

"Lead the way, husband. I'm with you."

Her words earned her a quick kiss. He took her hand, both of them furtively sneaking to get their coats, the guests too absorbed in their own good time to notice.

"Henley," Joel said to the driver who stood in the entryway. "Would you drive us home?"

"Very good, sir. And may I offer my congratulations."

"Thank you."

"Home?" Clemmie looked at him strangely as they hurried into the brisk air. Henley opened the door to the Rolls, and Joel helped her inside. "I thought you rented a room at the hotel."

"Hush." He winked and hurried around to the other side of the car.

During the drive, he held her hand, at times bringing it to his mouth to kiss it, but he wouldn't answer her questions as to their destination. When the car reached Herbert's street, she groaned.

"Oh, Joel. Not the shed."

He laughed outright. "What kind of husband would I

be to take my new wife to spend our first night together in a box?"

She flushed with warmth at his words and smiled. "Actually, I'd stay anywhere with you. Be it your box of a shed or a fancy hotel."

"Oh good. Well, in that case. . ."

"Joel." She laughed. "Don't you dare!"

The chauffeur drove past Herbert's home and stopped two houses down the street.

"What?" Clemmie pulled her brows together. "Why are we stopping here?"

Joel didn't wait for Henley, hurrying out of the car to come around and help her to the sidewalk. She raised the hem of her long gown, taking his hand as he helped her over an icy puddle.

"Thank you, Henley. We can take it from here."

"Very good, sir."

Clemmie watched in confusion as the chauffeur drove away then turned to her new husband.

"Explain yourself, Joel Litton."

"Open your eyes and look," he said while taking hold of her shoulders and turning her to see the SOLD sign in the front yard.

Clemmie blinked as realization dawned. "Joel, you didn't. . ." He barely made enough at the paper. She turned to him. "I meant what I said. I'd live with you anywhere. Even your shed."

"Shhh." He placed his finger against her lips, sending a tingle down her spine. "I didn't. This is a wedding gift from your grandfather. I didn't want to accept, but he seemed hurt when I wouldn't, and I wasn't about to make you live in that shed."

"So you buried your pride to make an old man happy and ensure that we have a good place to live at a time when such things like homes are hard to come by," she said in wonder, realizing just how far Joel had come for a man who refused handouts.

"It was a gift. And he's family."

Clemmie's smile grew wide. "Joel Litton, have I told you how much I love you?"

He swept her off her feet, making her squeal, and held her close.

"Mrs. Litton, let me show you just how much I love you. I've been waiting for this day a long time."

His words partly took away her breath.

"Joel, you have no idea how long I've waited for you. Is this truly real?"

"Let's find out." His kiss finished the job his words had started. "Yeah," he whispered. "It's real."

Breathless with the emotions he'd sparked inside her—from ecstasy at becoming his wife to eagerness at fully belonging to him—she clung to her first and only love as he carried her over the threshold of their new home and into the start of their life together.

epilogue

Six months later

"Oh, aren't you the fussy one?"

Thea tended to her baby, putting him over her shoulder to burp him, while Clemmie made sandwiches for the girls. Loretta and Bethany sat at the table, drinking their milk and giggling over their pretend game of being mamas, one of their dolls in a chair between them.

"There you two go." Clemmie set their lunches in front of them. "And if you eat every bit, we have cookies for dessert."

"Yay!" Loretta squealed. "Chocowit chip?"

"Of course."

Clemmie's answer produced another squeal.

"You're good with the girls," Thea said. "With little Rupert, too. You'll make a fine mother one day."

Clemmie flushed with warmth. "I had plenty of experience at the refuge, taking care of my brothers and sisters and even some of the reformers."

"Strange name, that."

Clemmie shrugged. "It's what they chose to be called. Once-upon-a-time hooligans learning to better themselves so they can reform the world."

"Well, when you put it that way, I like it! It's catchy."

"I can't take the credit. That's Hannah's line. She's started writing plays for amusement and comes up with witty little slogans all the time."

Thea patted Rupert's back, smoothing circles over it. "I can't tell you how thrilled I am that we're neighbors. It's swell to be able to chat anytime with you, living only two houses away."

"I agree. That house can feel empty while Joel's at work. I'm used to a big family." The winter had been lonesome in the hours without him, and with the arrival of spring and warmer weather, Clemmie visited Thea's when her own housework was done.

The cat suddenly made a beeline for the door. Loretta jumped from her chair to let her outside and squealed. "Daddy and Uncle Joel are home!"

Clemmie quickly untied her apron and hurried outdoors to greet her husband.

"Hello, Herbert." She nodded then turned her full attention to the man of her dreams. "Joel."

She smiled, moving into his arms to give him a welcoming hug and kiss.

"Where's my wife?" Herbert complained. "I want some of that, too."

"Rupert's being fussy." At that moment, Thea appeared at the door, the baby in her arms. With a smile, Herbert went to his wife and embraced her.

"Let's go home," Clemmie suggested.

"All right."

They waved to their friends and walked to their house, whose front Clemmie planned to soon brighten with lilac bushes. Inside, Joel took her in his arms for a real kiss, scrambling her thoughts and her breath.

"How is my darling Clementine today?"

"Swell. Are you hungry?"

"Only for you."

His words and the light in his eyes left no doubt what he meant, making her go warm inside. Before he so delightfully diverted her from her mission, she wanted to say what she'd waited to say for hours.

"There's something I need to tell you."

"Mmm?" He touched his lips to hers again, trailing little kisses from her mouth to her jaw and her ear. "Did you know your hair shines like fire in the sun?" he whispered. His fingers wove into the strands as she struggled to think clearly.

"I had an appointment today."

"With the hairdresser? Don't change the color, Clemmie." Another kiss to her neck. "I know you've never been happy with it and talked of going platinum, but I love my feisty carrottop."

"It's not orange, it's almost auburn, and I didn't see a beautician. I went to a doctor."

He froze and moved to look at her. "Are you sick?"

"I'll be much better this coming winter. But before that, we need to decorate the spare room. Perhaps with a theme of fluffy little bunnies?"

He shook his head in confusion.

"Honestly, Joel." She smiled, wrapping her arms around his neck. "Your senses may have sharpened when you were blind, but sometimes you can be so dull. You might have two carrot-tops come December, could even be on my birthday—so, what do you think of that?"

His eyes widened in sudden comprehension. "You mean. . ."

"Yes." She giggled at his dazed reaction. She'd never known him to be at such a loss for words. "We're going to have a little carrottop. And I'm so glad you accepted Grandfather's gift, because with three of us, it might have gotten crowded in that box of a shed."

At that, Joel laughed and scooped her up, holding her tightly against him, his arms around her waist. She looked down at him, clutching his strong shoulders.

"You *are* happy then?" she asked softly.

"I can't think of news that would make me happier. Hot dog! I'm gonna be a father." He said the words as if he could scarcely believe them.

"Yes. The start of the big family I've always dreamed of. I want as many children—more—than my parents had. A dozen at least."

"A dozen? Hmm." Joel's eyes twinkled. "Well, sweetheart, you might be getting that wish sooner than you think."

"What do you mean?"

"Did I ever mention twins run in my family?"

Clemmie's eyes widened with shock. "You're teasing me again, right?"

His eyebrows lifted high, his blue eyes dancing, his smile wide.

"You *are* teasing."

Joel laughed and kissed her soundly, soon scattering all her thoughts and making her forget all else but this man she loved. . .

Her dream come true.

A Letter To Our Readers

Dear Reader:

In order that we might better contribute to your reading enjoyment, we would appreciate your taking a few minutes to respond to the following questions. We welcome your comments and read each form and letter we receive. When completed, please return to the following:

Fiction Editor
Heartsong Presents
PO Box 719
Uhrichsville, Ohio 44683

1. Did you enjoy reading *In Search of a Dream* by Pamela Griffin?
   ❏ Very much! I would like to see more books by this author!
   ❏ Moderately. I would have enjoyed it more if

   _____

   _____

   _____

2. Are you a member of **Heartsong Presents**? ❏ Yes ❏ No
   If no, where did you purchase this book? _____

   _____

3. How would you rate, on a scale from 1 (poor) to 5 (superior), the cover design? _____

4. On a scale from 1 (poor) to 10 (superior), please rate the following elements.

   _____ Heroine   _____ Plot
   _____ Hero   _____ Inspirational theme
   _____ Setting   _____ Secondary characters

5. These characters were special because? _____
_____
_____

6. How has this book inspired your life? _____
_____
_____

7. What settings would you like to see covered in future
   Heartsong Presents books? _____
_____
_____

8. What are some inspirational themes you would like to see
   treated in future books? _____
_____
_____

9. Would you be interested in reading other **Heartsong
   Presents** titles? ❏ Yes ❏ No

10. Please check your age range:
    ❏ Under 18   ❏ 18-24
    ❏ 25-34   ❏ 35-45
    ❏ 46-55   ❏ Over 55

Name _____
Occupation _____
Address _____
City, State, Zip _____
E-mail _____

SILVER MOUNTAINS

3 stories in 1

There siblings seek treasure and find it in faith and love. Can God show these siblings where true treasures lies?

Historical, paperback, 368 pages, 5¾₆" x 8"

Please send me ____ copies of *Silver Mountains*. I am enclosing $7.99 for each. (Please add $4.00 to cover postage and handling per order. OH add 7% tax. If outside the U.S. please call 740-922-7280 for shipping charges.)

Name _____

Address _____

City, State, Zip_____

To place a credit card order, call 1-740-922-7280.
Send to: Heartsong Presents Readers' Service, PO Box 721, Uhrichsville, OH 44683

Heart♥ong

HISTORICAL ROMANCE IS CHEAPER BY THE DOZEN!

Any 12 Heartsong Presents titles for only $27.00*

Buy any assortment of twelve *Heartsong Presents* titles and save 25% off of the already discounted price of $2.97 each!

*plus $4.00 shipping and handling per order and sales tax where applicable. If outside the U.S. please call 740-922-7280 for shipping charges.

HEARTSONG PRESENTS TITLES AVAILABLE NOW:

___HP675 *Bayou Secrets*, K. M. Y'Barbo
___HP676 *Beside Still Waters*, T. V. Bateman
___HP679 *Rose Kelly*, J. Spaeth
___HP680 *Rebecca's Heart*, L. Harris
___HP683 *A Gentleman's Kiss*, K. Comeaux
___HP684 *Copper Sunrise*, C. Cox
___HP687 *The Ruse*, T. H. Murray
___HP688 *A Handful of Flowers*, C. M. Hake
___HP691 *Bayou Dreams*, K. M. Y'Barbo
___HP692 *The Oregon Escort*, S. P. Davis
___HP695 *Into the Deep*, L. Bliss
___HP696 *Bridal Veil*, C. M. Hake
___HP699 *Bittersweet Remembrance*, G. Fields
___HP700 *Where the River Flows*, I. Brand
___HP703 *Moving the Mountain*, Y. Lehman
___HP704 *No Buttons or Beaux*, C. M. Hake
___HP707 *Mariah's Hope*, M. J. Conner
___HP708 *The Prisoner's Wife*, S. P. Davis
___HP711 *A Gentle Fragrance*, P. Griffin
___HP712 *Spoke of Love*, C. M. Hake
___HP715 *Vera's Turn for Love*, T. H. Murray
___HP716 *Spinning Out of Control*, V. McDonough
___HP719 *Weaving a Future*, S. P. Davis
___HP720 *Bridge Across the Sea*, P. Griffin
___HP723 *Adam's Bride*, L. Harris
___HP724 *A Daughter's Quest*, L. N. Dooley
___HP727 *Wyoming Hoofbeats*, S. P. Davis
___HP728 *A Place of Her Own*, L. A. Coleman
___HP731 *The Bounty Hunter and the Bride*, V. McDonough
___HP732 *Lonely in Longtree*, J. Stengl
___HP735 *Deborah*, M. Colvin
___HP736 *A Time to Plant*, K. E. Hake
___HP740 *The Castaway's Bride*, S. P. Davis
___HP741 *Golden Dawn*, C. M. Hake

___HP743 *Broken Bow*, I. Brand
___HP744 *Golden Days*, M. Connealy
___HP747 *A Wealth Beyond Riches*, V. McDonough
___HP748 *Golden Twilight*, K. Y'Barbo
___HP751 *The Music of Home*, T. H. Murray
___HP752 *Tara's Gold*, L. Harris
___HP755 *Journey to Love*, L. Bliss
___HP756 *The Lumberjack's Lady*, S. P. Davis
___HP759 *Stirring Up Romance*, J. L. Barton
___HP760 *Mountains Stand Strong*, I. Brand
___HP763 *A Time to Keep*, K. E. Hake
___HP764 *To Trust an Outlaw*, R. Gibson
___HP767 *A Bride Idea*, Y. Lehman
___HP768 *Sharon Takes a Hand*, R. Dow
___HP771 *Canteen Dreams*, C. Putman
___HP772 *Corduroy Road to Love*, L. A. Coleman
___HP775 *Treasure in the Hills*, P. W. Dooly
___HP776 *Betsy's Return*, W. E. Brunstetter
___HP779 *Joanna's Adventure*, M. J. Conner
___HP780 *The Dreams of Hannah Williams*, L. Ford
___HP783 *Seneca Shadows*, L. Bliss
___HP784 *Promises, Promises*, A. Miller
___HP787 *A Time to Laugh*, K. Hake
___HP788 *Uncertain Alliance*, M. Davis
___HP791 *Better Than Gold*, L. A. Eakes
___HP792 *Sweet Forever*, R. Cecil
___HP795 *A Treasure Reborn*, P. Griffin
___HP796 *The Captain's Wife*, M. Davis
___HP799 *Sandhill Dreams*, C. C. Putman
___HP800 *Return to Love*, S. P. Davis
___HP803 *Quills and Promises*, A. Miller
___HP804 *Reckless Rogue*, M. Davis
___HP807 *The Greatest Find*, P. W. Dooly
___HP808 *The Long Road Home*, R. Druten

(If ordering from this page, please remember to include it with the order form.)

Presents

Great Inspirational Romance at a Great Price!

Heartsong Presents books are inspirational romances in contemporary and historical settings, designed to give you an enjoyable, spirit-lifting reading experience. You can choose wonderfully written titles from some of today's best authors like Wanda E. Brunstetter, Mary Connealy, Susan Page Davis, Cathy Marie Hake, Joyce Livingston, and many others.

When ordering quantities less than twelve, above titles are $2.97 each.
Not all titles may be available at time of order.

SEND TO: **Heartsong Presents** Readers' Service
            P.O. Box 721, Uhrichsville, Ohio 44683

Please send me the items checked above. I am enclosing $ _____
(please add $4.00 to cover postage per order. OH add 7% tax. WA
add 8.5%). Send check or money order, no cash or C.O.D.s, please.
      To place a credit card order, call 1-740-922-7280.

NAME _____

ADDRESS _____

CITY/STATE _____ ZIP_____

                                            HPS 7-10

HEARTSONG
PRESENTS

If you love Christian romance...

 $10.⁹⁹

You'll love Heartsong Presents' inspiring and faith-filled romances by today's very best Christian authors. . .Wanda E. Brunstetter, Mary Conneoly, Susan Page Davis, Cathy Marie Hake, and Joyce Livingston, to mention a few!

When you join Heartsong Presents, you'll enjoy four brand-new, mass-market, 176-page books—two contemporary and two historical—that will build you up in your faith when you discover God's role in every relationship you read about!

Mass Market 176 Pages

Imagine. . .four new romances every four weeks—with men and women like you who long to meet the one God has chosen as the love of their lives...all for the low price of $10.99 postpaid.

To join, simply visit www.heartsong presents.com or complete the coupon below and mail it to the address provided.

- -

YES! Sign me up for Heartso♥ng!

NEW MEMBERSHIPS WILL BE SHIPPED IMMEDIATELY!
Send no money now. We'll bill you only $10.99 postpaid with your first shipment of four books. Or for faster action, call 1-740-922-7280.

NAME _____

ADDRESS_____

CITY_____ STATE _____ ZIP _____

MAIL TO: HEARTSONG PRESENTS, P.O. Box 721, Uhrichsville, Ohio 44683
or sign up at WWW.HEARTSONGPRESENTS.COM